Chronicles of Carlingford. The Perpetual Curate.

Vol. 3

SALZWASSER
VERLAG

Margaret Oliphant

Chronicles of Carlingford. The Perpetual Curate.

Vol. 3

Reprint of the original, first published in 1864.

1st Edition 2022 | ISBN: 978-3-75259-364-8

Verlag (Publisher): Salzwasser Verlag GmbH, Zeilweg 44, 60439 Frankfurt, Deutschland
Vertretungsberechtigt (Authorized to represent): E. Roepke, Zeilweg 44, 60439 Frankfurt, Deutschland
Druck (Print): Books on Demand GmbH, In de Tarpen 42, 22848 Norderstedt, Deutschland

THE

PERPETUAL CURATE

Chronicles of Carlingford

THE

PERPETUAL CURATE

BY THE

AUTHOR OF 'SALEM CHAPEL,' ETC.

IN THREE VOLUMES

VOL. III.

MDCCCLXIV

Chronicles of Carlingford.

THE PERPETUAL CURATE.

CHAPTER XXXVI.

THE first investigation into the character of the Rev. F. C. Wentworth, Curate of St Roque's, was fixed to take place in the vestry of the parish church, at eleven o'clock on the morning of the day which followed this anxious night. Most people in Carlingford were aware that the Perpetual Curate was to be put upon his trial on that sunny July morning; and there was naturally a good deal of curiosity among the intelligent townsfolk to see how he looked, and what was the aspect of the witnesses who were to bear testimony for or against him. It is always interesting to the crowd to see how a man looks at a great crisis of his life—or a woman either, for that matter; and if a human creature, at the height of joy, or in the depths of sorrow, is a spectacle to draw everybody's eyes, there is a still greater dramatic interest in the sight when hope and fear are both in action, and the alternative hangs between life or death. It was life or death to Mr Wentworth, though the tribunal was one which could inflict no penalties. If he should be found guilty, death would be a light doom to the downfall and moral extinction which would make an end of the unfaithful priest; and, consequently, Carlingford had reason for its curiosity. There was a crowd about the back entrance which led to the shabby little sacristy where Mr Morgan and Mr Leeson were accustomed to robe themselves; and scores of people strayed into the church itself, and hung about, pretending to look at the improvements which the Rector called restorations. Mrs Morgan herself, looking very pale, was in and out half-a-dozen times in the hour, talking with terrible science and technicalism to Mr Finial's clerk of works, who could not make her see that she was talking Gothic—a language which had nothing to do with Carlingford Church, that building being of the Revolution or churchwarden epoch. She was a great deal too much agitated at that moment to be aware of the distinction. As for Mr Wentworth, it was universally agreed that, though he looked a little flushed and excited, there was no particular discouragement visible in his face. He went in to the vestry with some eagerness, not much like a culprit on his trial. The Rector, indeed, who was heated and embarrassed and doubtful of himself, looked more like a criminal than the real hero. There were six of the amateur judges, of whom one had felt his heart fail him at the last moment. The five who were steadfast were Mr Morgan, Dr Marjoribanks, old Mr Western (who was a distant cousin of the Wodehouses, and brother-in-law, though old enough to be her grandfather, of the beautiful Lady Western, who once lived in Grange Lane), and with them Mr Centum, the banker, and old Colonel Chiley. Mr Proctor, who was very uneasy in his mind, and much afraid lest he should be called upon to give an account of the Curate's behaviour on the previous night, had added himself as a kind of auxiliary to this judicial bench. Mr Waters had volunteered his services as counsellor, perhaps with the intention of looking after the interests of a very different client; and to this imposing assembly John Brown had walked in, with his hands in his pockets, rather disturbing the composure of the company in general, who were aware what kind of criticism his was. While the bed of justice was being arranged, a very odd little group collected in the outer room, where Elsworthy, in a feverish state of excitement, was revolving about the place from the door to the window, and where the Miss Hemmings sat up against the wall, with their drapery drawn up about them, to show that they were of different clay from Mrs Elsworthy, who, respectful but sullen, sat on the same bench. The anxious public peered in at the door whenever it had a chance, and took peeps through the window when the other privilege was impossible. Besides the Miss Hemmings and the Elsworthys there was Peter Hayles, who also had seen something, and the wife of another shopkeeper at the end of George Street; and there was the Miss Hemmings' maid, who had escorted them on that eventful night of Rosa's disappearance. Not one of the witnesses had the smallest doubt as to the statement he or she was about to make; they were entirely convinced of the righteousness of their own cause, and the justice of the accusation, which naturally gave a wonderful moral force to their testimony. Besides — but that was quite a different matter — they all had their little grudges against Mr Wentworth, each in his secret heart.

When Elsworthy was called in to the inner room it caused a little commotion amid this company outside. The Miss Hemmings looked at each other, not with an agreeable expression of face. "They might have had the politeness to call us first," Miss Sophia said to her sister; and Miss Hemmings shook her head and sighed, and said, "Dear Mr Bury!" an observation which meant a great deal, though it did not seem perfectly relevant. "Laws! I'll forget everythink when I'm took in there," said the shopkeeper's wife to Miss Hemmings' maid; and the ladies drew still closer up, superior to curiosity, while the others stretched their necks to get a peep into the terrible inner room.

It was indeed a formidable tribunal. The room was small, so that the unfortunate witness was within the closest range of six pairs of judicial eyes, not to speak of the vigilant orbs of the two lawyers, and those of the accused and his supporters. Mr Morgan, by right of his position, sat at the end of the table, and looked very severely at the first witness as he came in—which Elsworthy did, carrying his hat before him like a kind of shield, and polishing it carefully round and round. The Rector was far from having any intention of discouraging the witness, who was indeed his mainstay; but the anxiety of his peculiar position, as being at once counsel for the prosecution, and chief magistrate of the bed of justice, gave an unusual sternness to his face.

"Your name is George Elsworthy," said the Rector, filling his pen with ink, and looking penetratingly in the witness's face.

"George Appleby Elsworthy," said Rosa's uncle, a little alarmed; "not as I often signs in full; for you see, sir, it's a long name, and life's short, and it ain't necessary in the way of business——"

"Stationer and newsmonger in Carlingford," interrupted the Rector; "I should say in Upper Grange Lane, Carlingford; aged——?"

"But it doesn't appear to me that newsmonger is a correct expression," said old Mr Western, who was very conversational; "newsmonger means a gossip, not a tradesman; not that there is any reason why a tradesman should not be a gossip, but——"

"Aged?" said Mr Morgan, holding his pen suspended in the air. "I will say newsvendor if that will be better—one cannot be too particular—Aged——?"

"He is come to years of discretion," said Dr Marjoribanks, "that's all we need; don't keep us all day waiting, man, but tell your story about this elopement of your niece. When did it take place, and what are the facts? Never mind your hat, but say out what you have got to say."

"You are much too summary, Doctor," said Mr Morgan, with a little offence; but the sense of the assembly was clearly with Dr Marjoribanks—so that the Rector dashed in 45 as the probable age of the witness, and waited his further statement.

After this there was silence, and Elsworthy began his story. He narrated all the facts of Rosa's disappearance, with an intention and bias which made his true tale a wonderful tacit accusation. Rage, revenge, a sense of wrong, worked what in an indifferent narrator only the highest skill could have wrought. He did not mention the Curate's name, but arranged all his facts in lines like so many trains of artillery. How Rosa was in the habit of going to Mrs Hadwin's (it was contrary to Elsworthy's instinct to bring in at this moment any reference to Mr Wentworth) every night with the newspaper—"not as I sent her of errands for common—keeping two boys for the purpose," said the injured man; "but, right or wrong, there's where she'd go as certain as the night come. I've seen her with my own eyes go into Mrs Hadwin's garden-door, which she hadn't no need to go in but for being encouraged; and it would be half an hour at the least afore she came out."

"But, bless me! that was very imprudent of you," cried Mr Proctor, who up to this time had not uttered a word.

"There was nobody there but the old lady and her maids—except the clergyman," said Elsworthy. "It wasn't my part to think as she could get any harm from the clergyman. She wouldn't hear no remonstrances from me; she *would* go as regular as the evening come."

"Yes, yes," said Mr Waters, who saw John Brown's humorous eye gleaming round upon the little assembly; "but let us come to the immediate matter in hand. Your niece disappeared from Carlingford on the ——?"

"Yes, yes," said Mr Western, "we must not sink into conversation; that's the danger of all unofficial investigations. It seems natural to let him tell his story as he likes; but here we have got somebody to keep us in order. It's natural, but it ain't law—is it, Brown?"

"I don't see that law has anything to do with it," said John Brown, with a smile.

"Order! order!" said the Rector, who was much goaded and aggravated by this remark. "I request that there may be no conversation. The witness will proceed with what he has to say. Your niece disappeared on the 15th. What were the circumstances of her going away?"

"She went down as usual with the newspaper," said Elsworthy; "it had got to be a custom as regular as regular. She stopped out later nor common, and my wife and me was put out. I don't mind saying, gentlemen," said the witness, with candour, "as my missis and I wasn't altogether of the same mind about Rosa. She was late, but I can't say as I was anxious. It wasn't above a week afore that Mr Wentworth himself brought her home safe, and it was well known as he didn't like her to be out at night; so I was easy in my mind, like. But when eleven o'clock came, and there was no denying of its being past hours, I began to get a little fidgety. I stepped out to the door, and I looked up and down, and saw nobody; so I took up my hat and took a turn down the road——"

At this moment there was a little disturbance outside. A voice at which the Curate started was audible, asking entrance. "I must see Mr Wentworth immediately," this voice said, as the door was partially opened; and then, while his sons both rose to their feet, the Squire himself suddenly entered the room. He looked round upon the assembled company with a glance of shame and grief that went to the Curate's heart. Then he bowed to the judges, who were looking at him with an uncomfortable sense of his identity, and walked across the room to the bench on which Gerald and Frank were seated together. "I beg your pardon, gentlemen," said the Squire, "if I interrupt your proceedings; but I have only this moment arrived in Carlingford, and heard what was going on, and I trust I may be allowed to remain, as my son's honour is concerned." Mr Wentworth scarcely waited for the assent which everybody united in murmuring, but seated himself heavily on the bench, as if glad to sit down anywhere. He suffered Frank to grasp his hand, but scarcely gave it; nor, indeed, did he look, except once, with a bitter momentary glance at the brothers. They were sons a father might well have been proud of, so far as external appearances went; but the Squire's soul was bitter within him. One was about to abandon all that made life valuable in the eyes of the sober-minded country gentleman. The other——"And I could have sworn by Frank," the mortified father was saying in his heart. He sat down with a dull, dogged composure. He meant to hear it all, and have it proved to him that his favourite son was a villain. No wonder that he was disinclined to respond to any courtesies. He set himself down almost with impatience that the sound of his entrance should have interrupted the narrative, and looked straight in front of him, fixing his eyes on Elsworthy, and taking no notice of the anxious glances of the possible culprit at his side.

"I hadn't gone above a step or two when I see Mr Hayles at his door. I said to him, 'It's a fine evening,'—as so it was, and the stars shining. 'My Rosa ain't been about your place, has she?' I says; and he says, 'No.' But, gentlemen, I see by the look of his eye as he had more to say. 'Ain't she come home yet?' says Mr Hayles——"

"Stop a moment," said John Brown. "Peter Hayles is outside, I think. If the Rector wishes to preserve any sort of legal form in this inquiry, may I suggest that a conversation repeated is not evidence? Let Elsworthy tell what he knows, and the other can speak for himself——"

"It is essential we should hear the conversation," said the Rector, "since I believe it was of importance. I believe it is an important link in the evidence—I believe——"

"Mr Morgan apparently has heard the evidence before," said the inexorable John Brown.

Here a little commotion arose in the bed of justice. "Hush, hush," said Dr Marjoribanks; "the question is, What has the witness got to say of his own knowledge? Go on, Elsworthy; we can't possibly spend the whole day here. Never mind what Hayles said, unless he communicated something about the girl."

"He told me as the Miss Hemmings had seen Rosa," said Elsworthy, slowly; "had seen her at nine, or half after nine—I won't be sure which—at Mrs Hadwin's gate."

"The Miss Hemmings are outside. Let the Miss Hemmings be called," said Mr Proctor, who had a great respect for Mr Brown's opinion.

But here Mr Waters interposed. "The Miss Hemmings will be called presently," he said; "in the mean time let this witness be heard out; afterwards his evidence will be corroborated. Go on, Elsworthy."

"The Miss Hemmings had seen my Rosa at Mrs Hadwin's gate," repeated Elsworthy, "a-standing outside, and Mr Wentworth a-standing inside; there ain't more respectable parties in all Carlingford. It was them as saw it, not me. Gentlemen, I went back home. I went out again. I went over all the town a-looking for her. Six o'clock in the morning come, and I had never closed an eye, nor took off my clothes, nor even sat down upon a chair. When it was an hour as I could go to a gentleman's house and no offence, I went to the place as she was last seen. Me and Mr Hayles, we went together. The shutters was all shut but on one window, which was Mr Wentworth's study. We knocked at the garden-door, and I ain't pretending that we didn't make a noise; and, gentlemen, it wasn't none of the servants

—it was Mr Wentworth hisself as opened the door."

There was here a visible sensation among the judges. It was a point that told. As for the Squire, he set his stick firmly before him, and leaned his clasped hands upon it to steady himself. His healthful, ruddy countenance was paling gradually. If it had been an apostle who spoke, he could not have taken in more entirely the bitter tale.

"It was Mr Wentworth hisself, gentlemen," said the triumphant witness; "not like a man roused out of his sleep, but dressed and shaved, and his hair brushed, as if it had been ten instead o' six. It's well known in Carlingford as he ain't an early man; and gentlemen here knows it as well as me. I don't pretend as I could keep my temper. I give him my mind, gentlemen, being an injured man; but I said as —if he do his duty by her——"

"Softly a moment," said Mr Brown. "What had Mr Wentworth's aspect at six o'clock in the morning to do with Rosa Elsworthy's disappearance at nine on the previous night?"

"I don't see that the question is called for at the present moment," said Mr Waters. "Let us hear what reasons you have for attributing to Mr Wentworth an unusual degree of interest in your niece."

"Sir," said Elsworthy, "he come into my shop as regular as the day; he never come but he asked after Rosa, or spoke to her if she was there. One night he walked all the way up Grange Lane and knocked at my door and brought her in all of a glow, and said I wasn't to send her out late no more. My missis, being a woman as is very particular, was struck, and thought as harm might come of it; and, not to be talked of, we sent Rosa away. And what does Mr Wentworth do, but the moment he hears of it comes right off to my shop! He had been at his own home, sir, a-visiting his respected family," said Elsworthy, turning slightly towards the side of the room where the father and sons sat together. "He came to my shop with his carpet-bag as he come off the railway, and he gave me my orders as I was to bring Rosa back. What he said was, 'Directly,' that very day. I never had no thought but what his meaning was honourable—being a clergyman," said the witness, with a heavy sigh; and then there ensued a little pause.

"The Miss Hemmings had better be called now," said Mr Waters. "Elsworthy, you can retire; but we may require you again, so you had better not go away. Request Miss Hemmings to do us the favour of coming here."

The Squire lifted his heavy eyes when the next witness entered. She made a very solemn curtsy to the gentlemen, and sat down on the chair which somebody placed for her. Being unsupported, a lady—not to say an unmarried lady profoundly conscious of the fact—among a number of men, Miss Hemmings was naturally much agitated. She was the eldest and the softest-hearted; and it occurred to her for the first time, as she gave a frightened look towards the Curate, that he was like her favourite younger brother, who had died ever so many ages ago—a thought which, for the first time, made her doubtful of her testimony, and disposed to break down in her evidence.

"You were in Grange Lane on the evening of the 15th ultimo," said Mr Morgan, after he had carefully written down her name, "about nine o'clock?"

"Oh yes, Mr Morgan," said the poor lady; "we were at St Roque's Cottage drinking tea with Mrs Bland, who was lodging with Mrs Smith in the same rooms Mrs Rider used to have. I put the note of invitation in my pocket in case there should be any doubt; but, indeed, poor Mrs Bland was taken very ill on the 16th, and Dr Marjoribanks was called, and he knows it could not be any other evening—and besides——"

"About nine o'clock," said Mr Waters; "did I understand you, it was about nine o'clock?"

"She was such an invalid, poor dear," said Miss Hemmings, apologetically; "and it is such a privilege to have real Christian conversation. We dined early on purpose, and we were asked for half-past six. I think it must have been a little after nine; but Mary is here, and she knows what hour she came for us. Shall I call Mary, please?"

"Presently," said the counsel for the prosecution. "Don't be agitated; one or two questions will do. You passed Mrs Hadwin's door coming up. Will you kindly tell the gentlemen what you saw there?"

"Oh!" cried Miss Hemmings. She looked round at the Curate again, and he was more than ever like Willie who died. "I—I don't take much notice of what I see in the streets," she said, faltering; "and there are always so many poor people going to see Mr Wentworth." Here the poor lady stopped short. She had never considered before what harm her evidence might do. Now her heart smote her for the young man who was like Willie. "He is so very kind to all the poor people," continued the unwilling witness, looking doubtfully round into all the faces near her; "and he's such a young man," she added, in her tremulous way. It was Miss Sophia who was strong-minded; all the poor women in Back Grove Street were perfectly aware that their chances were doubled when they found Miss Jane.

"But you must tell us what you saw all the same," said Dr Marjoribanks. "I daresay Mr Wentworth wishes it as much as we do."

The Curate got up and came forward with one of his impulses. "I wish it a great deal more," he said. "My dear Miss Hemmings, thank you for your reluctance to say anything to harm me; but the truth can't possibly harm me: tell them exactly what you saw."

Miss Hemmings looked from one to another, and trembled more and more. "I am sure I never meant to injure Mr Wentworth," she said; "I only said I thought it was imprudent of him—that was all I meant. Oh, I am sure, if I had thought of this, I would rather have done anything than say it. And whatever Sophia might have imagined, I assure you, gentlemen, *I* never, never for a moment thought Mr Wentworth meant any harm."

"Never mind Mr Wentworth," said Mr Brown, who now took the matter in hand. "When you were passing Mrs Hadwin's house about nine o'clock on the evening of the 15th, you saw some one standing at the door. Mr Wentworth particularly wishes you to say who it was."

"Oh, Mr Brown—oh, Mr Morgan," cried the poor lady; "it was little Rosa Elsworthy. She was a designing little artful thing. When she was in my Sunday class, she was always thinking of her vanities. Mr Wentworth was talking to her at the garden-door. I daresay he was giving her good advice; and oh, gentlemen, if you were to question me for ever and ever, that is all I have got to say."

"Did you not hear what they were talking about?" said Mr Proctor. "If it was good advice——" The late Rector stopped short, and grew red, and felt that his supposition was that of a simpleton. "You heard what they were talking about? What did they say?" he concluded, peremptorily, in a tone which frightened the reluctant witness more and more.

"I did not hear a single word," she cried—"not a word. That is all I know about it. Oh, please, let me go away. I feel very faint. I should like a little cold water, please. I did not hear a word—not a word. I have told you everything I have got to say."

Everybody looked more serious when Miss Hemmings stumbled from her chair. She was so frightened at her own testimony, and so unwilling to give it, that its importance was doubled in the eyes of the inexperienced judges. The Squire gave a low groan under his breath, and turned his eyes, which had been fixed upon her, on the ground instead; but raised them immediately, with a gleam of anxiety, as his son again rose from his side. All that the Curate meant to do was to give the trembling lady his arm, and lead her out; but the entire assembly, with the exception of John Brown, started and stared as if he had been about to take instant revenge upon the frightened woman. Miss Hemmings burst into tears when Mr Wentworth set a chair for her by the door, and brought her a glass of water, in the outer room; and just then somebody knocked and gave him a note, with which he returned to the presence of the awful tribunal. Miss Sophia Hemmings was corroborating her sister's statement when the Perpetual Curate re-entered. He stood behind her quite quietly, until she had finished, with a slight smile upon his lip, and the note in his hand. Dr Marjoribanks was not partial to Miss Sophia Hemmings. She was never ill herself, and rarely permitted even her sister to enjoy the gentle satisfaction of a day's sickness. The old Doctor looked instead at the Perpetual Curate. When Miss Hemmings withdrew, Dr Marjoribanks interposed. "It appears to me that Mr Wentworth has something to say," said the Doctor. "It is quite necessary that he should have a hearing as well as the rest of us. Let Peter Hayles wait a moment, till we hear what Mr Wentworth has to say."

"It is not yet time for us to receive Mr Wentworth's statement," said the Rector. "He shall certainly be heard in his own defence at the proper time. Mr Waters, call Peter Hayles."

"One moment," said the Curate. "I have no statement to make, and I can wait till you have heard what everybody has to say, if the Rector wishes it; but it might save time and trouble to hear me. I have another witness whom, up to this moment, I have been reluctant to bring forward—a witness all-important for me, whom I cannot produce in so public a place, or at an hour when everybody is abroad. If you will do me the favour to adjourn this inquiry till the evening, and to meet then in a private house—in my own, or Miss Wentworth's, or wherever you may appoint—I think I can undertake to make this whole business perfectly clear."

"Bless me!" said Mr Proctor, suddenly. This unexpected and irrelevant benediction was the first sound distinctly audible in the little stir of surprise, expectation, and excitement which followed the Curate's speech. The Squire let his stick fall out of his hands, and groped after it to pick it up again. Hope had suddenly all at once come into possession of the old man's breast. As for the Rector, he was too much annoyed at the moment to speak.

"You should have thought of this before," said Dr Marjoribanks. "It would have been just as easy to fix this meeting for the evening, and in a private house, and would have saved time. You are very welcome to my dining-room, if you please; but I don't understand why it could not have been settled so at once, and saved our time," said the Doctor; to which sentiment there were several murmurs of assent.

"Gentlemen," said the Curate, whose eyes were sparkling with excitement, "you must all know in your hearts that this trial ought never to have taken place. I have lived among you for five years, and you ought to have known me by this time. I have never been asked for an explanation, neither could any explanation which it was possible for me to make have convinced a mind prejudiced against me," he said, after a moment's pause, with a meaning which everybody understood. "It is only now that I feel myself able to clear up the whole matter; and it is for this reason alone that I ask you to put off your inquiry till to-night."

"I don't feel inclined to consent to any adjournment," said Mr Morgan; "it looks like an attempt to defeat the ends of justice." The Rector was very much annoyed—more than he dared confess to himself. He believed in his heart that young Wentworth was guilty, and he felt equally convinced that here was some unexpected loophole through which he would escape. But public opinion was strong in Grange Lane—stronger than a new Rector. The Banker and the Doctor and the Indian Colonel, not to speak of old Mr Western, were disposed to grant the request of the Curate; and when even Mr Proctor forsook his side, the Rector himself yielded. "Though it is against my judgment," he said, "and I see no advantage to be gained by it, the meeting had better be held in the Rectory, this evening at seven o'clock."

"Most of us dine at seven o'clock," said Dr Marjoribanks.

"This evening at eight o'clock," said the Rector, severely. "I will request all the witnesses to be in attendance, and we must hope to find Mr Wentworth's witness of sufficient importance to justify the change. At eight o'clock this evening, in my house, gentlemen," said the Rector. He collected his notes and went outside, and began talking to his witnesses, while the others collected together round the table to consult over this new phase of the affair. The three Mr Wentworths went out together, the father between his two tall sons. The Squire's strength was much shaken, both in mind and body. When they were out of the shadow of the church, he looked up in Frank's face.

"I hope you consider me entitled to an immediate explanation," said Mr Wentworth. "When I read that anonymous letter, it went a long way towards breaking my heart, sir; I can tell you it did. Jack here too, and your brother making up his mind as he has done, Frank. I am not a man to complain. If it were all over with me to-morrow, I shouldn't be sorry, so far as I am concerned, if it weren't for the girls and the little children. But I always thought I could have sworn by Frank," said the old man, mournfully. He was ever so much older since he had said these words before in the long lime avenue at Wentworth Hall.

CHAPTER XXXVII.

The little assembly which met in the vestry of Carlingford Church to inquire into the conduct of the Perpetual Curate, had so many different interests in hands when it dispersed, and so much to do, that it is difficult for the narrator of this history to decide which thread should be taken up first. Of all the interlocutors, however, perhaps Mr Proctor was the one who had least succeeded in his efforts to explain himself, and accordingly demands in the first place the attention of an impartial historian. The excellent man was still labouring under much perplexity when the bed of justice was broken up. He began to recollect that Mr Wentworth's explanation on the previous night had convinced him of his innocence, and to see that it was indeed altogether inconceivable that the Curate should be guilty; but then, other matters still more disagreeable to contemplate than Mr Wentworth's guilt came in to darken the picture. This vagabond Wodehouse, whom the Curate had taken in at his sister's request—what was the meaning of that mystery? Mr Proctor had never been anyhow connected with mysteries; he was himself an only son, and had lived a straightforward peaceable life. Neither he nor his estimable parents, so far as the late Rector was aware, had ever done anything to be ashamed of; and he winced a little at the thought of connecting himself with concealment and secrecy. And then the Curate's sudden disappearance on the previous evening perplexed and troubled him. He imagined all kinds of reasons for it as he walked down Grange Lane. Perhaps Miss Wodehouse, who would not receive himself, had sent for Mr Wentworth; perhaps the vagabond brother was in some other scrape, out of which he had to be extricated by the Curate's assistance. Mr Proctor was perfectly honest, and indeed determined, in his "intentions;" but everybody will allow that for a middle-aged lover of fifty or thereabouts, contemplating a sensible match with a lady of suitable years and means, to find suddenly that the object of his affections was not only a penniless woman, but the natural guardian of an equally penniless sister, was startling, to say the least of it. He was a true man, and it did not occur to him to decline the responsibility altogether; on the contrary, he was perhaps more eager than he would have been otherwise, seeing that his elderly love had far more need of his devotion than he had ever expected her to have; but, notwithstanding, he was disturbed by such an unlooked-for change of circumstances, as was natural, and did not quite know what was to be done with Lucy. He was full of thoughts on this subject as he proceeded towards the house, to the interview which, to use sentimental language, was to decide his fate. But, to tell the truth, Mr Proctor was not in a state of very deep anxiety about his fate. The idea of being refused was too unreasonable an idea to gain much ground in his mind. He was going to offer his personal support, affection, and sympathy to Miss Wodehouse at the least fortunate moment of her life; and if there was anything consolatory in marriage at all, the late Rector sensibly concluded that it must be doubly comforting under such circumstances, and that the offer of an honest man's hand and house and income was not a likely thing to be rejected by a woman of Miss

Wodehouse's experience and good sense—not to speak of his heart, which was very honest and true and affectionate, though it had outlived the fervours of youth. Such was Mr Proctor's view of the matter; and the chances were strong that Miss Wodehouse entirely agreed with him—so, but for a certain shyness which made him rather nervous, it would not be correct to say that the late Rector was in a state of special anxiety about the answer he was likely to receive. He was, however, anxious about Lucy. His bachelor mind was familiar with all the ordinary traditions about the inexpediency of being surrounded by a wife's family; and he had a little of the primitive male sentiment, shared one way or other by most husbands, that the old system of buying a woman right out, and carrying her off for his own sole and private satisfaction, was, after all, the correct way of managing such matters. To be sure, a pretty, young, unmarried sister, was perhaps the least objectionable encumbrance a woman could have; but, notwithstanding, Mr Proctor would have been glad could he have seen any feasible way of disposing of Lucy. It was utterly out of the question to think of her going out as a governess; and it was quite evident that Mr Wentworth, even were he perfectly cleared of every imputation, having himself nothing to live upon, could scarcely offer to share his poverty with poor Mr Wodehouse's cherished pet and darling. "I daresay she has been used to live expensively," Mr Proctor said to himself, wincing a little in his own mind at the thought. It was about one o'clock when he reached the green door—an hour at which, during the few months of his incumbency at Carlingford, he had often presented himself at that hospitable house. Poor Mr Wodehouse! Mr Proctor could not help wondering at that moment how he was getting on in a world where, according to ordinary ideas, there are no lunch nor dinner parties, no old port nor savoury side-dishes. Somehow it was impossible to realise Mr Wodehouse with other surroundings than those of good-living and creature-comfort. Mr Proctor sighed, half for the departed, half at thought of the strangeness of that unknown life for which he himself did not feel much more fitted than Mr Wodehouse. In the garden he saw the new heir sulkily marching about among the flower-beds smoking, and looking almost as much out of place in the sweet tranquillity of the English garden, as a churchwarden of Carlingford or a Fellow of All-

Souls could look, to carry out Mr Proctor's previous imagination, in the vague beatitude of a disembodied heaven. Wodehouse was so sick of his own company that he came hastily forward at the sight of a visitor, but shrank a little when he saw who it was.

"I suppose you have brought some news," he said, in his sullen way. "I suppose he has been making his statements, has he? Much I care! He may tell what lies he pleases; he can't do me any harm. I never did anything but sign my own name, by Jove! Jack Wentworth himself says so. I don't care *that* for the parson and his threats," said Wodehouse, snapping his fingers in Mr Proctor's face. The late Rector drew back a little, with a shudder of disgust and resentment. He could not help thinking that this fellow would most likely be his brother-in-law presently, and the horror he felt made itself visible in his face.

"I am quite unaware what you can mean," said Mr Proctor. "I am a parson, but I never made any threats that I know of. I wish to see Miss Wodehouse. I—I think she expects me at this hour," he said, with a little embarrassment, turning to John, who, for his part, had been standing by in a way which became his position as a respectable and faithful servant, waiting any opportunity that might come handy to show his disgust for the new *régime*.

"Yes, sir," said John, promptly, and with emphasis. "My mistress expects you, sir. She's come down to the drawing-room for the first time. Miss Lucy keeps her room, sir, still; she's dreadfully cut up, poor dear young lady. My mistress will be glad to see you, sir," said John. This repetition of a title which Miss Wodehouse had not been in the habit of receiving was intended for the special advantage of the new master, whom John had no intention of recognising in that capacity. "If you should know of any one, sir, as is in want of a steady servant," the man continued, as he led the way into the house, with a shrewd glance at Mr Proctor, whose "intentions" were legible enough to John's experienced eyes—"not as I'm afeared of getting suited, being well known in Carlingford; but it would come natural to be with a friend of the family. There ain't a servant in the house, sir, as will stay when the ladies go, and I think as Miss Wodehouse would speak for me," said John, with natural astuteness. This address made Mr Proctor a little uneasy. It recalled to him the unpleasant side of the important transaction in which he was about to engage. He was not rich, and did not see his way now to any near prospect of requiring the services of "a steady servant," and the thought made him sigh.

"We'll see," he said, with a troubled look. To persevere honourably in his "intentions" was one thing, but to be insensible to the loss of much he had looked forward to was quite another. It was accordingly with a grave and somewhat disturbed expression that he went to the interview which was "to decide his fate." Miss Wodehouse was seated in the drawing-room, looking slightly flushed and excited. Though she knew it was very wrong to be thus roused into a new interest the day after her father's funeral, the events altogether had been of so startling a description that the usual decorum of an afflicted household had already been ruthlessly broken. And, on the whole, notwithstanding her watching and grief, Mr Proctor thought he had never seen the object of his affections looking so well as she did now in the long black dress, which suited her better than the faint dove colours in which she arrayed herself by preference. She was not, it is true, quite sure what Mr Proctor wanted in this interview he had solicited, but a certain feminine instinct instructed her in its probable eventualities. So she sat in a subdued flutter, with a little colour fluctuating on her cheek, a tear in her eyes, and some wonder and expectation in her heart. Perhaps in her youth Miss Wodehouse might have come to such a feminine crisis before; but if so, it was long ago, and the gentle woman had never been given to matrimonial speculations, and was as fresh and inexperienced as any girl. The black frame in which she was set made her soft colour look fresher and less faded. Her plaintive voice, the general softness of her demeanour, looked harmonious and suitable to her circumstances. Mr Proctor, who had by no means fallen in love with her on account of any remnants of beauty she might possess, had never admired her so much as he did now; he felt confused, good man, as he stood before her, and, seeing her so much younger and fairer than his former idea, began to grow alarmed, and wonder at his serenity. What if she thought him an old fogey? what if she refused him? This supposition brought a crimson colour to Mr Proctor's middle-aged countenance, and was far from restoring his courage. It was a wonderful relief to him when she, with the instinct of a timid woman, rushed into hasty talk.

"It was very kind of you to come yesterday," she said; "Lucy and I were very grateful. We have not many relatives, and my dear father——"

"Yes," said the late Rector, again embarrassed by the tears which choked her voice, "he was very much respected: that must be a consolation to you. And he had a long life—and—and I suppose, on the whole, a happy one," said Mr Proctor, "with you and your sister——"

"Oh, Mr Proctor, he had a great deal to put up with," said Miss Wodehouse, through her tears. She had, like most simple people, an instinctive disinclination to admit that anybody was or had been happy. It looked like an admission of inferiority. "Mamma's death, and poor Tom," said the elder sister. As she wiped her eyes, she almost forgot her own little feminine flutter of expectancy in respect to Mr Proctor himself. Perhaps it was not going to happen this time, and as she was pretty well assured that it would happen one day or another, she was not anxious about it. "If I only knew what to do about Tom," she continued, with a vague appeal in her voice.

Mr Proctor got up from his chair and walked to the window. When he had looked out he came back, rather surprising Miss Wodehouse by his unlooked-for movements. "I wanted very much to have a little conversation with you," he said, growing again very red. "I daresay you will be surprised—but I have accepted another living, Miss Wodehouse;" and here the good man stopped short in a terrible state of embarrassment, not knowing what next to say.

"Yes?" said Miss Wodehouse, interrogatively. Her heart began to beat quicker, but perhaps he was only going to tell her about the new work he had undertaken; and then she was a woman, and had some knowledge, which came by nature, how to conduct herself on an occasion such as this.

"I don't know whether you recollect," said Mr Proctor—"I shall never forget it—one time when we all met in a house where a woman was dying,—I mean your sister and young Wentworth, and you and I;—and neither you nor I knew anything about it," said the late Rector, in a strange voice. It was not a complimentary way of opening his subject, and the occurrence had not made so strong an impression upon Miss Wodehouse as upon her companion. She looked a little puzzled, and, as he made a pause, gave only a murmur of something like assent, and waited to hear what more he might have to say.

"We neither of us knew anything about it," said Mr Proctor—"neither you how to manage her, nor I what to say to her, though the young people did. I have always thought of you from that time. I have thought I should like to try whether I was good for anything now—if you would help me," said the middle-aged lover. When he had said this he walked to the window, and once more looked out, and came back redder than ever. "You see we are neither of us young," said Mr Proctor; and he stood by the table turning over the books nervously, without looking at her, which was certainly an odd commencement for a wooing.

"That is quite true," said Miss Wodehouse, rather primly. She had never disputed the fact by word or deed, but still it was not pleasant to have the statement thus thrust upon her without any apparent provocation. It was not the sort of thing which a woman expects to have said to her under such circumstances. "I am sure I hope you will do better—I mean be more comfortable—this time," she continued, after a pause, sitting very erect on her seat.

"If you will help me," said Mr Proctor, taking up one of the books and reading the name on it, which was lucky for him, for it was Miss Wodehouse's name, which he either had forgotten or never had known.

And here they came to a dead stop. What was she to say? She was a little affronted, to tell the truth, that he should remember more distinctly than anything else her age, and her unlucky failure on that one occasion. "You have just said that I could not manage," said the mild woman, not without a little vigour of her own; "and how then could I help you, Mr Proctor? Lucy knows a great deal more about parish work than I do," she went on in a lower tone; and for one half of a second there arose in the mind of the elder sister a kind of wistful half envy of Lucy, who *was* young, and knew how to manage—a feeling which died in unspeakable remorse and compunction as soon as it had birth.

"But Lucy would not have me," said the late Rector; "and indeed I should not know what to do with her if she would have me;—but you—— It is a small parish, but it's not a bad living. I should do all I could to make you comfortable. At least we might try," said Mr Proctor, in his most insinuating tone. "Don't you think we might try? at least it would do——" He was going to say "no harm," but on second thoughts rejected that expression. "At least I should be very glad if you would," said the excellent man, with renewed confusion. "It's a nice little rectory, with a pretty garden, and all that sort of thing; and—and perhaps—it might help you to settle about going away—and—and I daresay there would be room for Lucy. Don't you think you would try?" cried Mr Proctor, volunteering, in spite of himself, the very hospitality which he had thought it hard might be required of him; but somehow his suit seemed to want backing at the actual moment when it was being made.

As for Miss Wodehouse, she sat and listened to him till he began to falter, and then her composure gave way all at once. "But as for trying," she gasped, in broken mouthfuls of speech, "that would never—never do, Mr Proctor. It has to be done—done for good and all—if—if it is done at all," sobbed the poor lady, whose voice came somewhat muffled through her handkerchief and her tears.

"Then it shall be for good and all!" cried Mr Proctor, with a sudden impulse of energy. This was how it came about that Miss Wodehouse and the late Rector were engaged. He had an idea that he might be expected to kiss her, and certainly ought to call her Mary after this; and hovered for another minute near her seat, not at all disinclined for the former operation. But his courage failed him, and he only drew a chair a little closer and sat down, hoping that she would soon stop crying. And indeed, by the time that he produced out of his pocketbook the little photograph of the new rectory, which he had had made for her by a rural artist, Miss Wodehouse had emerged out of her handkerchief, and was perhaps in her heart as happy in a quiet way as she had ever been in her life. She who had never been good for much, was now, in the time of their need, endowed with a home which she could offer Lucy. It was she, the helpless one of the family, who was to be her young sister's deliverer. Let it be forgiven to her if, in the tumult of the moment, this was the thought that came first.

When Miss Wodehouse went up-stairs after this agitating but satisfactory interview, she found Lucy engaged in putting together some books and personal trifles of her own which were scattered about the little sitting-room. She had been reading 'In Memoriam' until it vexed her to feel how inevitably good sense came in and interfered with the enthusiasm of her grief, making her sensible that to apply to her fond old father all the lofty lauds which were appropriate to the poet's hero would be folly indeed. He had been a good tender father to her, but he was not "the sweetest soul that ever looked with human eyes;" and Lucy could not but stop in her reading with a kind of pang and self-reproach as this consciousness came upon her. Miss Wodehouse looked rather aghast when she found her sister thus occupied. "Did you think of accepting Miss Wentworth's invitation, after all?" said Miss Wodehouse; "but, dear, I am afraid it would be awkward; and oh, Lucy, my darling, I have so many things to tell you," said the anxious sister, who was shy of communicating her own particular news. Before many minutes had passed, Lucy had thrown aside all the books, and was sitting by her sister's side in half-pleased, disconcerted amazement to hear her story. Only half pleased—for Lucy, like most other girls of her age, thought love and marriage were things which belonged only to her own level of existence, and was a little vexed and disappointed to find that her elder sister could condescend to such youthful matters. On the whole, she rather blushed for Mary, and felt sadly as if she had come down from an imaginary pedestal. And then Mr Proctor, so old and so ordinary, whom it was impossible to think of as a bridegroom, and still less as a brother. "I shall get used to it presently," said Lucy, with a burning flush on her cheek, and a half feeling that she had reason to be ashamed; "but it is so strange to think of you in that way, Mary. I always thought you were too—too sensible for that sort of thing," which was a reproach that went to Miss Wodehouse's heart.

"Oh, Lucy dear," said that mild woman, who in this view of the matter became as much ashamed of herself as Lucy could desire, "what could I do? I know what you mean, at my time of life; but I could not let you be dependent on Tom, my darling," said Miss Wodehouse, with a deprecating appealing look.

"No indeed," said Lucy; "that would be impossible under any circumstances: nor on you either, Mary dear. I can do something to make a living, and I should like it. I have always been fond of work. I will not permit you to sacrifice yourself for me," said the younger sister, with some dignity. "I see how it has been. I felt sure it was not of your own accord."

Miss Wodehouse wrung her hands with dismay and perplexity. What was she to do if Lucy stood out and refused her consent? She could not humble herself so far as to confess that she rather liked Mr Proctor, and was, on the whole, not displeased to be married; for the feeling that Lucy expected her to be too sensible for that sort of thing overawed the poor lady. "But, Lucy, I have given him my promise," said poor Miss Wodehouse. "It—it would make him very unhappy. I can't use him badly, Lucy dear."

"I will speak to him, and explain if it is necessary. Whatever happens, I can't let you sacrifice yourself for me," said Lucy. All the answer Miss Wodehouse could make was expressed in the tears of vexation and mortification which rushed to her eyes. She repelled her young sister's ministrations for the first time in her life with hasty impatience. Her troubles had not been few for the last twenty-four hours. She had been questioned about Tom till she had altogether lost her head, and scarcely knew what she was saying; and Lucy had not applauded that notable expedient of throwing the shame of the family upon Mr Wentworth, to be concealed and taken care of, which had brought so many vexations to the Perpetual Curate. Miss Wodehouse at last was driven to bay. She had done all for the best, but nobody gave her any credit for it; and now this last step, by which she had meant to provide a home for Lucy, was about to be contradicted and put a stop to altogether. She put away Lucy's arm, and rejected her consolations. "What is the use of pretending to be fond of me if I am always to be wrong, and never to have my—my own way in anything?" cried the poor lady, who, beginning with steadiness, broke down before she reached the end of her little speech. The words made Lucy open her blue eyes with wonder; and after that there followed a fuller explanation, which greatly changed the ideas of the younger sister. After her "consent" had been at last extracted from her, and when Miss Wodehouse regained her composure, she reported to Lucy the greater part of the conversation which had taken place in the drawing-room, of which Mr Proctor's proposal constituted only a part, and which touched upon matters still more interesting to her hearer. The two sisters, preoccupied by their father's illness and death, had up to this time but a vague knowledge of the difficulties which surrounded the Perpetual Curate. His trial, which Mr Proctor had reported to his newly-betrothed, had been unsuspected by either of them; and they were not even aware of the event which had given rise to it—the disappearance of Rosa Elsworthy. Miss Wodehouse told the story with faltering lips, not being able to divest herself of the idea that, having been publicly accused, Mr Wentworth must be more or less guilty; while, at the same time, a sense that her brother must have had something to do with it, and a great reluctance to name his name, complicated the narrative. She had already got into trouble with Lucy about this unlucky brother, and unconsciously, in her story, she took an air of defence. "I should have thought better of Mr

Wentworth if he had not tried to throw the guilt on another," said the perplexed woman. "Oh, Lucy dear, between two people it is so hard to know what to do."

"I know what I shall do," said Lucy, promptly; but she would not further explain herself. She was, however, quite roused up out of 'In Memoriam.' She went to her desk and drew out some of the paper deeply edged with black, which announced before words its tale of grief to all her correspondents. It was with some alarm that Miss Wodehouse awaited this letter, which was placed before her as soon as finished. This was what, as soon as she knew the story, Lucy's prompt and generous spirit said—

"Dear Mr Wentworth,—We have just heard of the vexations you have been suffering, to our great indignation and distress. Some people may think it is a matter with which I have no business to interfere; but I cannot have you think for a moment that we, to whom you have been so kind, could put the slightest faith in any such accusations against you. We are not of much consequence, but we are two women, to whom any such evil would be a horror. If it is any one connected with us who has brought you into this painful position, it gives us the more reason to be indignant and angry. I know now what you meant about the will. If it was to do over again, I should do just the same; but for all that, I understand now what you meant. I understand also how much we owe to you, of which, up to yesterday, I was totally unaware. You ought never to have been asked to take our burden upon your shoulders. I suppose you ought not to have done it; but all the same, thank you with all my heart. I don't suppose we ever can do anything for you to show our gratitude; and indeed I do not believe in paying back. But in the mean time, thank you—and don't, from any consideration for us, suffer a stain which belongs to another to rest upon yourself. You are a clergyman, and your reputation must be clear. Pardon me for saying so, as if I were qualified to advise you; but it would be terrible to think that you were suffering such an injury out of consideration for us.—Gratefully and truly yours,

LUCY WODEHOUSE."

The conclusion of this letter gave Lucy a good deal of trouble. Her honest heart was so moved with gratitude and admiration that she had nearly called herself "affectionately" Mr Wentworth's. Why should not she? "He has acted like a brother to us," Lucy said to herself; and then she paused to inquire whether his conduct had indeed arisen from brotherly motives solely. Then, when she had begun to write "faithfully" instead, a further difficulty occurred to her. Not thus lightly and unsolicited could she call herself "faithful," for did not the word mean everything that words could convey in any human relationship? When she had concluded it at last, and satisfied her scruples by the formula above, she laid the letter before her sister. This event terminated the active operations of the day in the dwelling of the Wodehouses. Their brother had not asked to see them, had not interrupted them as yet in their retreat up-stairs, where they were sedulously waited upon by the entire household. When Miss Wodehouse's agitation was over, she too began to collect together her books and personalities, and they ended by a long consultation where they were to go and what they were to do, during the course of which the elder sister exhibited with a certain shy pride that little photograph of the new rectory, in which there was one window embowered in foliage, which the bride had already concluded was to be Lucy's room. Lucy yielded during this sisterly conference to sympathetic thoughts even of Mr Proctor. The two women were alone in the world. They were still so near the grave and the deathbed that chance words spoken without thought from time to time awakened in both the ready tears. Now and then they each paused to consider with a sob what *he* would have liked best. They knew very little of what was going on outside at the moment when they were occupied with those simple calculations. What was to become of them, as people say—what money they were to have, or means of living—neither was much occupied in thinking of. They had each other; they had, besides, one a novel and timid middle-aged confidence, the other an illimitable youthful faith in one man in the world. Even Lucy, whose mind and thoughts were more individual than her sister's, wanted little else at that moment to make her happy with a tender tremulous consolation in the midst of her grief.

CHAPTER XXXVIII.

While matters were thus arranging themselves in the ideas at least of the two sisters whose prospects had been so suddenly changed, explanations of a very varied kind were going on in the house of the Miss Wentworths. It was a very full house by this time, having been invaded and taken possession of by the "family" in a way which entirely obliterated the calmer interests and occupations of the habitual inhabitants. The three ladies had reached that stage of life which knows no personal events except those of illness and death; and the presence of Jack Wentworth, of Frank and Gerald, and even of Louisa, reduced them altogether to the rank of spectators, the audience, or at the utmost the chorus, of the drama; though this was scarcely the case with Miss Dora, who kept her own room, where she lay on the sofa, and received visits, and told the story of her extraordinary adventure, the only adventure of her life. The interest of the household centred chiefly, however, in the dining-room, which, as being the least habitable apartment in the house, was considered to be most adapted for anything in the shape of business. On the way from the church to Miss Wentworth's house the Curate had given his father a brief account of all the events which had led to his present position; but though much eased in his mind, and partly satisfied, the Squire was not yet clear how it all came about. His countenance was far from having regained that composure, which indeed the recent course of events in the family had pretty nearly driven out of his life. His fresh light-coloured morning dress, with all its little niceties, and the fresh colour which even anxiety could not drive away from his cheeks, were somehow contradicted in their sentiment of cheerfulness by the puckers in his forehead and the harassed look of his face. He sat down in the big leathern chair by the fireplace, and looked round him with a sigh, and the air of a man who wonders what will be the next vexation. "I'd like to hear it over again, Frank," said the Squire. "My mind is not what it used to be:

I don't say I ever was clever, like you young fellows, but I used to understand what was said to me. Now I seem to require to hear everything twice over; perhaps it is because I have had myself to say the same things over again a great many times lately," he added, with a sigh of weariness. Most likely his eye fell on Gerald as he said so; at all events, the Rector of Wentworth moved sadly from where he was standing and went to the window, where he was out of his father's range of vision. Gerald's looks, his movements, every action of his, seemed somehow to bear a symbolic meaning at this crisis in his life. He was no longer in any doubt; he had made up his mind. He looked like a martyr walking to his execution, as he crossed the room; and the Squire looked after him, and once more breathed out of his impatient breast a heavy short sigh. Louisa, who had placed herself in the other great chair at the other side of the forlorn fireplace, from which, this summer afternoon, there came no cheerful light, put up her handkerchief to her eyes and began to cry with half-audible sobs — which circumstances surrounding him were far from being encouraging to Frank as he entered anew into his own story—a story which he told with many interruptions. The Squire, who had once "sworn by Frank," had now a terrible shadow of distrust in his mind. Jack was here on the spot, of whom the unfortunate father knew more harm than he had ever told, and the secret dread that he had somehow corrupted his younger brother came like a cold shadow over Mr Wentworth's mind. He could not slur over any part of the narrative, but cross-examined his son to the extent of his ability, with an anxious inquisition into all the particulars. He was too deeply concerned to take anything for granted. He sat up in his chair with those puckers in his forehead, with that harassed look in his eyes, making an anxious, vigilant, suspicious investigation, which was pathetic to behold. If the defendant, who was thus being examined on his honour, had been guilty, the heart of the judge would have broken; but that was all the more reason for searching into it with jealous particularity, and with a suspicion which kept always gleaming out of his troubled eyes in sudden anxious glances, saying, "You are guilty? Are you guilty?" with mingled accusations and appeals. The accused, being innocent, felt this suspicion more hard to bear than if he had been a hundred times guilty.

"I understand a little about this fellow Wodehouse," said the Squire; "but what I want to know is, why you took him in? What did you take him in for, sir, at first? Perhaps I could understand the rest if you would satisfy me of that."

"I took him in," said the Curate, rather slowly, "because his sister asked me. She threw him upon my charity—she told me the danger he was in——"

"What danger was he in?" asked the Squire.

The Curate made a pause, and as he paused Mr Wentworth leaned forward in his chair, with another pucker in his forehead and a still sharper gleam of suspicion in his eyes. "His father had been offended time after time in the most serious way. This time he had threatened to give him up to justice. I can't tell you what he had done, because it would be breaking my trust—but he had made himself obnoxious to the law," said Frank Wentworth. "To save him from the chance of being arrested, his sister brought him to me."

The Squire's hand shook a good deal as he took out his handkerchief and wiped his forehead. "Perhaps it would be the best way if one had not too much regard for the honour of the family," he said, tremulously, like a man under a sudden temptation; "but the sister, sir, why did she bring him to you?" he added, immediately after, with renewed energy. Mr Wentworth was not aware that, while he was speaking, his eldest son had come into the room. He had his back to the door, and he did not see Jack, who stood rather doubtfully on the threshold, with a certain shade of embarrassment upon his ordinary composure. "It is not everybody that a woman would confide her brother's life to," said the Squire. "Who is the sister? Is she—is there any—any entanglement that I don't know of? It will be better for all of us if you tell me plainly," said the old man, with a querulous sound in his voice. He forgot the relationship of his own girls to Jack, and groaned within himself at what appeared almost certain evidence that the sister of a criminal like Wodehouse had got possession of Frank.

"Miss Wodehouse is about the same age as my aunt Dora," said the Curate. It was an exaggeration which would have gone to the poor lady's heart, but Frank Wentworth, in the unconscious insolence of his youth, was quite unaware and careless of the difference. Then he paused for a moment with an involuntary smile. "But I am a clergyman, sir," he continued, seriously. "If a man in my position is good for anything, it is his business to help the helpless. I could do no good in any other way —I took him into my house."

"Frank," said the Squire, "I beg your pardon. I believe in my heart you're true and honest. If I were not driven out of my senses by one thing and another," said Mr Wentworth, with bitterness. "They make me unjust to you, sir —unjust to you! But never mind; go on. Why didn't you tell these fellows what you've told me? That would have settled the business at once, without any more ado."

"Mr Morgan is a great deal too much prejudiced against me to believe anything I said. I thought it better to let him prove to himself his own injustice; and another still more powerful reason——" said the Curate.

"Stop, sir, stop; I can't follow you to more than one thing at a time. Why is Mr Morgan prejudiced against you?" said the Squire, once more sitting upright and recommencing his examination.

Frank Wentworth laughed in spite of himself,

though he was far from being amused. "I know no reason except that I have worked in his parish without his permission," he answered, briefly enough, "for which he threatened to have me up before somebody or other—Dr Lushington, I suppose, who is the new Council of Trent, and settles all our matters for us nowadays," said the Curate, not without a little natural scorn, at which, however, his father groaned.

"There is nothing to laugh at in Dr Lushington," said the Squire. "He gives you justice, at all events, which you parsons never give each other, you know. You ought not to have worked in the Rector's parish, sir, without his permission. It's like shooting in another man's grounds. However, that's not my business;—and the other reason, sir?" said Mr Wentworth, with his anxious look.

"My dear father," said the Curate, touched by the anxiety in the Squire's face, and sitting down by him with a sudden impulse, "I have done nothing which either you or I need be ashamed of. I am grieved that you should think it necessary to examine me so closely. Wodehouse is a rascal, but I had taken charge of him; and as long as it was possible to shield him, I felt bound to do so. I made an appeal to his honour, if he had any, and to his fears, which are more to be depended on, and gave him until noon to-day to consider it. Here is his note, which was given me in the vestry; and now you know the whole business, and how it is that I postponed the conclusion till to-night."

The Squire put on his spectacles with a tremulous hand to read the note which his son gave him. The room was very still while he read it, no sound interrupting him except an occasional sniff from Louisa, who was in a permanent state of whimpering, and, besides, had ceased to be interested in Frank's affairs. Jack Wentworth, standing in the background behind the Squire's chair, had the whole party before him, and studied them keenly with thoughts which nobody guessed at. Gerald was still standing by the window, leaning on it with his face only half turned to the others. Was he thinking of the others? was he still one of them? or was he saying his office from some invisible breviary abstracted into another life? That supposition looked the most like truth. Near him was his wife, who had thrown herself, a heap of bright fluttering muslin, into the great chair, and kept her handkerchief to her red eyes. She had enough troubles of her own to occupy her, poor soul! Just at that moment it occurred to her to think of the laburnum berries in the shrubbery at the Rectory, which, it was suddenly borne in upon her, would prove fatal to one or other of the children in her absence; — the dear Rectory which she had to leave so soon! "And Frank will have it, of course," Louisa said to herself, "and marry somebody;" and then she thought of the laburnum berries in connection with his problematical children, not without a movement of satisfaction. Opposite to her was the Squire, holding Wodehouse's epistle in a hand which shook a little, and reading aloud slowly as he could make it out. The note was short and insolent enough. While it was being read, Jack Wentworth, who was not easily discomposed, grew red and restless. He had not dictated it certainly, nor even suggested the wording of the epistle; but it was he who, half in scorn and half in pity of the vagabond's terrors, had reassured Wodehouse, and convinced him that it was only the punishments of public opinion which the Curate could bring upon him. Hardened as Jack was, he could not but be conscious that thus to stand in his brother's way was a shabby business enough, and to feel that he himself and his *protégé* cut a very poor figure in presence of the manful old Squire with all his burdens, and of Frank, who had, after all, nothing to explain which was not to his honour. Notwithstanding that he was at the present moment his brother's adversary, actually working against him and prolonging his difficulties, an odd kind of contempt and indignation against the fools who could doubt Frank's honour possessed the prodigal at the moment. "A parcel of asses," he said to himself; and so stood and listened to Wodehouse's little note of defiance, which, but for his prompting, the sullen vagabond would never have dared to send to his former protector. The letter itself was as follows:—

"I have consulted my friends about what you said to-day, and they tell me it is d—d nonsense. You can't do me any harm; and I don't mean to get myself into any scrape for you. You can do what you like—I shan't take any notice. Your love-affairs are no business of mine.—Yours truly,

"T. Wodehouse."

Mr Wentworth threw the miserable scrawl on the table. "The fellow is a scoundrel," said the Squire; "he does not seem to have a spark of gratitude. You've done a deal too much for him already; and if the sister is as old as Dora——" he continued, after a long pause, with a half-humorous relaxation of his features. He was too much worn out to smile.

"Yes," said the Curate. The young man was sensible of a sudden flush and heat, but did not feel any inclination to smile. Matters were very serious just then with Frank Wentworth. He was about to shake himself free of one vexation, no doubt; but at this moment, when Lucy Wodehouse was homeless and helpless, he had nothing to offer her, nor any prospects even which he dared ask her to share with him. This was no time to speak of the other sister, who was not as old as Miss Dora. He was more than ever the Perpetual Curate now. Perhaps, being a clergyman, he ought not to have been swayed by such merely human emotions; but honour and pride alike demanded that he should remain in Carlingford, and he had no shelter to offer Lucy in the time of her need.

After this there followed a pause, which was

far from being cheerful. Frank could not but be disconsolate enough over his prospects when the excitement died away; and there was another big, terrible event looming darkly in the midst of the family, which they had not courage to name to each other. The long, uneasy pause was at length broken by Louisa, whose voice sounded in the unnatural silence like the burst of impatient rain which precedes a thunderstorm.

"Now that you have done with Frank's affairs, if you have done with them," said Louisa, "perhaps somebody will speak to Gerald. I don't mean in the way of arguing. If some one would only speak *sense* to him. You all know as well as I do how many children we've got, and—and—an—other coming," sobbed the poor lady, "if something doesn't happen to me, which I am sure is more than likely, and might be expected. I don't blame dear grandpapa, for he has said everything, and so have I; but I do think his brothers ought to take a little more interest. Oh, Frank, you know it doesn't matter for you. You are a young man, you can go anywhere; but when there are five children and—and—an—other ——. And how are we to live? You know what a little bit of money I had when Gerald married me. Everybody knows Gerald never cared for money. If I had had a good fortune it would have been quite different," cried poor Louisa, with a little flow of tears and querulous sob, as though that too was Gerald's fault. "He has not sent off his letter yet, Frank," said the injured wife ; "if you would but speak to him. He does not mind me or grandpapa, but he might mind you. Tell him we shall have nothing to live on ; tell him——"

"Hush," said Gerald. He came forward to the table, very pale and patient, as became a man at the point of legal death. "I *have* sent away my letter. By this time I am no longer Rector of Wentworth. Do not break my heart. Do you think there is any particular in the whole matter which I have not considered —the children, yourself, everything? Hush ; there is nothing now to be said."

The Squire rose, almost as pale as his son, from his chair. "I think I'll go out into the air a little," said Mr Wentworth. "There's always something new happening. Here is a son of my own," said the old man, rising into a flush of energy, "who has not only deserted his post, but deserted it secretly, Frank. God bless my soul! don't speak to me, sir; I tell you he's gone over to the enemy as much as Charley would have done if he had deserted at the Alma—and done it when nobody knew or was thinking. I used to be thought a man of honour in my day," said Mr Wentworth, bitterly; "and it's a mean thing to say it came by their mother's side. There's Jack——"

The eldest son roused himself up at the mention of his own name. Notwithstanding all his faults, he was not a man to stand behind backs and listen to what was said of him. He came forward with his usual ease, though a close observer might have detected a flush on his face. "I am here, sir," said the heir. "I cannot flatter myself you will have much pleasure in seeing me; but I suppose I have still a right to be considered one of the family." The Squire, who had risen to his feet, and was standing leaning against the table when Jack advanced, returned to his chair and sat down as his eldest son confronted him. They had not met for years, and the shock was great. Mr Wentworth put his hand to his cravat and pulled at it with an instinctive movement. The old man was still feeble from his late illness, and apprehensive of a return of the disease of the Wentworths. He restrained himself, however, with force so passionate that Jack did not guess at the meaning of the gasp which, before the Squire was able to speak to him, convulsed his throat, and made Frank start forward to offer assistance which his father impatiently rejected. The Squire made, indeed, a great effort to speak with dignity. He looked from one to another of his tall sons as he propped himself up by the arms of his chair.

"You are the most important member of the family," said Mr Wentworth; "it is long since you have been among us, but that is not our fault. If things had been different, I should have been glad of your advice as a man of the world. Anyhow, I can't wish you to be estranged from your brothers," said the Squire. It was all any one could say. The heir of Wentworth was not to be denounced or insulted among his kindred, but he could not be taken to their bosom. Perhaps the reception thus given him was more galling than any other could have been to Jack Wentworth's pride. He stood at the table by himself before his father, feeling that there existed no living relations between himself and any one present. He had keen intellectual perceptions, and could recognise the beauty of honour and worth as well as most people; and the contrast between himself and the others who surrounded him presented itself in a very forcible light to Jack. Instead of Gerald and Frank, Wodehouse was *his* allotted companion. For that once he was bitter, notwithstanding his habitual good-humour.

"Yes," he said; "it would be a pity to estrange me from my brothers. We are, on the whole, a lucky trio. I, whom my relations are civil to; and Frank, who is not acquitted yet, though he seems so confident; and Gerald, who has made the greatest mistake of all——"

"Jack," said the Curate, "nobody wants to quarrel with you. You've dealt shabbily by me, but I do not mind. Only talk of things you understand—don't talk of Gerald."

For a moment Jack Wentworth was roused almost to passion. "What is Gerald that I should not understand him?" said Jack; "he and I are the original brood. You are all a set of interlopers, the rest of you. What is Gerald, that I should not talk of him? In the world, my dear Frank," continued the heir, superciliously, "as the Squire himself will testify, a man is not generally exempted from criticism because he is a parson. Gerald is——"

"I am a simple Catholic layman, nothing more," said Gerald; "not worth criticism, having done nothing. I am aware I am as good as dead. There is no reason why Jack should not talk if it pleases him. It will make no difference to me."

"And yet," said Frank, "it is only the other day that you told us you were nothing if not a priest."

Gerald turned upon him with a look of melancholy reproach that went to the Curate's heart. "It is true I said so," he replied, and then he made a pause, and the light died out of his pale face. "Don't bring up the ghosts of my dead battles, Frank. I said so only the other day. But it is the glory of the true Church," said the convert, with a sudden glow which restored colour for a moment to his face, "to restrain and subdue the last enemy, the will of man. I am content to be nothing, as the saints were. The fight has been hard enough, but I am not ashamed of the victory. When the law of the Church and the obedience of the saints ordain me to be nothing, I consent to it. There is nothing more to say."

"And this is how it is to be!" cried Louisa. "He knows what is coming, and he does not care—and none of you will interfere or speak to him! It is not as if he did not know what would happen. He tells you himself that he will be nothing; and even if *he* can put up with it after being a man of such consideration in the county, how am *I* to put up with it? We have always been used to the very best society," said poor Louisa, with tears. "The Duke himself was not more thought of; and now he tells you he is to be nothing!" Mrs Wentworth stopped to dry her eyes with tremulous haste. "*He* may not mind," said Louisa, "for at least he is having his own way. It is all very well for a man, who can do as he pleases; but it is his poor wife who will have to suffer. I don't know who will visit me after it's all over, and people will give over asking us if we don't ask them again; and how can we ever have anybody, with five children—or more—and only a few hundreds a-year? Oh, Frank, it kills me to think of it. Don't you think you might speak to him again?" she whispered, stretching up to his ear, when Gerald, with a sigh, had gone back to his window. The Squire, too, cast an appealing glance at his younger son.

"It is all true enough that she says," said

Mr Wentworth. "She mayn't understand *him*, Frank, but she's right enough in what she's saying. If things were different between your brother and me, I'd ask his advice," said the Squire, with a sigh. He gave a longing look at his eldest son, who stood with his usual ease before the fireplace. Matters had gone a great deal too far between the father and son to admit of the usual displeasure of an aggrieved parent—all that was over long ago; and Mr Wentworth could not restrain a certain melting of the heart towards his first-born. "He's not what I could wish, but he's a man of the world, and might give us some practical advice," said the Squire, with his anxious looks. Of what possible advantage advice, practical or otherwise, could have been in the circumstances, it was difficult to see; but the Squire was a man of simple mind, and still believed in the suggestions of wisdom. He still sat in the easy-chair, looking wistfully at Jack, and with a certain faith that matters might even yet be mended, if the counsel of his eldest son, as a man of the world, could be had and could be trusted; when Frank, who had an afternoon service at Wharfside, had to leave the family committee. Gerald, who roused up when his younger brother mentioned the business he was going upon, looked at Frank almost as wistfully as his father looked at Jack. "It may be the last time," he said to himself: "if you'll let me, I'll go with you, Frank;" and so the little conclave was broken up. The people in Prickett's Lane were greatly impressed by the aspect of Gerald Wentworth, as he went, silent and pale, by his brother's side, down the crowded pavement. They thought it must be a bishop at least who accompanied the Curate of St Roque's; and the women gathered at a little distance and made their comments, as he stood waiting for his brother after the service. "He don't look weakly nor sickly no more nor the clergyman," said one; "but he smiles at the little uns for all the world like my man smiled the night he was took away." "Smilin' or not smilin'," said another, "I don't see as it makes no matter; but I'd give a deal to know what Elsworthy and them as stands by Elsworthy can say after that." "Maybe, then, he'd give the poor fatherless children a blessing afore he'd go," suggested a poor Irish widow, who, having been much under Mr Wentworth's hands "in her trouble," was not quite sure now what faith she professed, or at least which Church she belonged to.

Such was the universal sentiment of Prickett's Lane. Meanwhile Gerald stood silent, and looked with pathetic, speechless eyes at the little crowd. He was no priest now—he was shorn of the profession which had been his life. His hope of being able to resign all things for Christ's sake had failed him. Too wary and politic to maintain in a critical age and country the old licence of the ages of Faith, even his wife's consent, could he have obtained it, would not have opened to the convert the way into the priesthood. A greater trial had been required of him; he was nothing, a man whose career was over. He stood idly, in a kind of languor, looking on while the Curate performed the duties of his office—feeling like a man whom sickness had reduced to the last stage of life, and for whom no earthly business remained; while, at the same time, his aspect struck awe, as that of a bishop at the least, to the imagination of Prickett's Lane.

CHAPTER XXXIX.

Mr Morgan did not go home direct from the investigation of the morning; on the contrary, he paid various visits, and got through a considerable amount of parish business, before he turned his face towards the Rectory. On the whole, his feelings were far from being comfortable. He did not know, certainly, who Mr Wentworth's witness was, but he had an unpleasant conviction that it was somebody who would clear the Curate. "Of course I shall be very glad," the Rector said to himself; but it is a fact, that in reality he was far from being glad, and that a secret conviction of this sentiment, stealing into his mind, made matters still more uncomfortable. This private sense of wishing evil to another man, of being unwilling and vexed to think well of his neighbour, was in itself enough to disturb the Rector's tranquillity; and when to this was added the aggravation that his wife had always been on the other side, and had warned him against proceeding, and might, if she pleased, say, "I told you so," it will be apparent that Mr Morgan's uneasiness was not without foundation. Instead of going home direct to acquaint his wife with the circumstances, about which he knew she must be curious, it was late in the afternoon before the Rector opened his own gate. Even then he went through the garden with a reluctant step, feeling it still more difficult to meet her now than it would have been at first, although his delay had arisen from the thought that it would be easier to encounter her keen looks after an interval. There was, however, no keen look to be dreaded at this moment. Mrs Morgan was busy with her ferns, and she did not look up as her husband approached. She went on with her occupation, examining carefully what withered fronds there might be about her favourite maidenhair, even when he stopped by her side. Though her husband's shadow fell across the plants she was tending, Mrs Morgan, for the first time in her married life, did not look up to welcome the Rector. She made no demonstration, said no word of displeasure, but only showed herself utterly absorbed in, and devoted to, her ferns. There was, to be sure, no such lover of ferns in the neighbourhood of Carlingford as the Rector's wife.

As for Mr Morgan, he stood by her side in a state of great discomfort and discomfiture. The good man's perceptions were not very clear, but he saw that she had heard from some one the issue of the morning's inquiry, and that she was deeply offended by his delay, and that, in short, they had arrived at a serious difference, the first quarrel since their marriage. Feeling himself in the wrong, Mr Morgan naturally grew angry too.

"I should like to have dinner earlier to-day," he said, with the usual indiscretion of an aggrieved husband. "Perhaps you will tell the cook, my dear. I think I should like to have it at five, if possible. It can't make much difference for one day."

Mrs Morgan raised herself up from her ferns, and no doubt it was a relief to her to find herself provided with so just a cause of displeasure. "Much difference!" cried the Rector's wife; "it is half-past four now. I wonder how you could think of such a thing, William. There is some lamb, which of course is not put down to roast yet, and the ducks. If you wish the cook to give warning immediately, you may send such a message. It is just like a man to think it would make no difference! But I must say, to do them justice," said the Rector's wife, "it is not like a man of your college!" When she had fired this double arrow, she took off her gardening gloves and lifted her basket. "I suppose you told Mr Proctor that you wished to dine early?" said Mrs Morgan, with severity, pausing on the threshold. "Of course it is quite impossible to have dinner at five unless he knows."

"Indeed I—I forgot all about Proctor," said the Rector, who now saw the inexpediency of his proposal. "On second thoughts, I see it does not matter much. But after dinner I expect some people about Mr Wentworth's business. It was not settled this morning, as I expected."

"So I heard," said Mrs Morgan. "I will tell Thomas to show them into the library," and she went indoors, carrying her basket. As for the Rector, he stood silent, looking after her, and feeling wonderfully discomfited. Had she found fault with him for his delay—had she even said,

"I told you so!" it would have been less overwhelming than this indifference. They had never had a quarrel before, and the effect was proportionately increased. After standing bewildered at the door for a few minutes, he retired into his study, where the change in his wife's demeanour haunted him, and obscured Mr Wentworth. Mrs Morgan sat at the head of the table at dinner with an equal want of curiosity. Even when the subject was discussed between the Rector and Mr Proctor, she asked no questions—a course of procedure very puzzling and trying to Mr Morgan, who could not make it out.

It was after eight o'clock before the tribunal of the morning was reconstituted at the Rectory. Most of the gentlemen came late, and the little assembly brought with it a flavour of port, which modified the serious atmosphere. When the bed of justice was again formed, Mr Wentworth entered with the body-guard of Wentworths, which numbered half as many as his judges. Half from curiosity, half from a reluctant inclination to please his father, Jack had joined the others, and they came in together, all of them noticeable men, profoundly different, yet identified as belonging to each other by the touching bond of family resemblance. After the four gentlemen had taken possession of their corner, Mr Waters made a somewhat hurried entry, bringing after him the sullen reluctant figure of Wodehouse, who made an awkward bow to the assembled potentates, and looked ashamed and vigilant, and very ill at ease. Mr Waters made a hasty explanation to the Rector before he sat down by the side of his unlucky client. "I thought it possible there might be some attempt made to shift the blame upon him, therefore I thought it best to bring him," said the lawyer. Mr Morgan gave him a dry little nod without answering. To tell the truth, the Rector felt anything but comfortable; when he glanced up at the stranger, who was looking askance at the people in the room as if they had been so many policemen in disguise, a disagreeable sudden conviction that this sullen rascal looked a great deal more like the guilty man than Mr Wentworth did, came into Mr Morgan's mind, and made him sick with annoyance and embarrassment. If it should turn out so! if it should become apparent that he, for private prejudices of his own, had been persecuting his brother! This thought produced an actual physical effect for the moment upon the Rector, but its immediate visible consequence was simply to make him look more severe, almost spiteful, in a kind of unconscious self-vindication. Last of all, Elsworthy, who began to be frightened too, but whose fears were mingled with no compunction nor blame of himself, stole in and found an uncomfortable seat on a stool near the door, where scarcely any one saw him, by favour of Thomas, and screened by the high back of the Rector's easy-chair. When all were assembled Mr Morgan spoke.

"We are met this evening, gentlemen, to complete, if there is sufficient time, the investigation we began this morning," said the Rector. "I have no doubt I express the sentiments of every one present when I say I shall be glad—*unfeignedly* glad," said Mr Morgan, with a defiant emphasis, which was meant to convince himself, "to find that Mr Wentworth's witness is of sufficient importance to justify the delay. As we were interrupted this morning solely on his account, I presume it will be most satisfactory that this witness should be called at once."

"I should like to say something in the first place," said the Curate. Mr Morgan made an abrupt nod indicative of his consent, and, instead of looking at the defendant, shaded his eyes with his hand, and made figures with his pen upon the blotting-paper. A conviction, against which it was impossible to strive, had taken possession of the Rector's soul. He listened to Frank Wentworth's address with a kind of impatient annoyance and resistance. "What is the good of saying any more about it?" Mr Morgan was saying in his soul. "For heaven's sake let us bury it and be done with it, and forget that we ever made such asses of ourselves." But at the same time the Rector knew this was quite impossible; and as he sat leaning over his blotting-book, writing down millions after millions with his unconscious pen, he looked a very model of an unwilling listener—a prejudiced judge—a man whom no arguments could convince; which was the aspect under which he appeared to the Curate of St Roque's.

"I should like to say something first," said the Perpetual Curate. "I could not believe it possible that I, being tolerably well known in Carlingford as I have always supposed, could be suspected by any rational being of such an insane piece of wickedness as has been laid to my charge; and consequently it did not occur to me to vindicate myself, as I perhaps ought to have done, at the beginning. I have been careless all along of vindicating myself. I had an idea," said the young man, with involuntary disdain, "that I might trust, if not to the regard, at least to the common sense of my friends——"

Here John Brown, who was near his unwary client, plucked at the Curate's coat, and brought him to a momentary half-angry pause. "Softly, softly," said Dr Marjoribanks; "common sense has nothing to do with facts; we're inquiring into facts at this moment; and, besides, it's a very foolish and unjustifiable confidence to trust to any man's common sense," said the old Doctor, with a humorous glance from under his shaggy eyebrows at his fellow-judges; upon which there ensued a laugh, not very agreeable in its tone, which brought the Rector to a white heat of impatience and secret rage.

"It appears to me that the witness ought to be called at once," said Mr Morgan, "if this is not a mere expedient to gain time, and if it is intended to make any progress to-night."

"My explanations shall be very brief," said Frank Wentworth, facing instantly to his natural enemy. "I have suspected from the beginning of this business who was the culprit, and have made every possible attempt to induce him to confess, and, so far as he could, amend the wrong that he had done. I have failed; and now the confession, the *amende*, must be made in public. I will now call my witness,' said the Curate. But this time a commotion rose in another part of the room. It was Wodehouse, who struggled to rise, and to get free from the detaining grasp of his companion.

"By Jove! I ain't going to sit here and listen to a parcel of lies!" cried the vagabond. "If I am to be tried, at least I'll have the real thing, by Jove!" He had risen up, and was endeavouring to pass Mr Waters and get out, casting a suspicious defiant look round the room. The noise he made turned all eyes upon him, and the scrutiny he had brought upon himself redoubled his anxiety to get away. "I'll not stand it, by Jove! Waters, let me go," said the craven, whose confused imagination had mixed up all his evil doings together, and who already felt himself being carried off to prison. It was at this moment that Jack Wentworth rose from his place in his easy careless way, and went forward to the table to adjust the lamp, which was flaring a little. Wodehouse dropped back into a chair as soon as he caught the eye of this master of his fate. His big beard moved with a subterranean gasp like the panting of a hunted creature, and all the colour that had remained died away out of his haggard, frightened face. As for Jack Wentworth, he took no apparent notice of the shabby rascal whom he held in awe. "Rather warm this room for a court of justice. I hope Frank's witness is not fat," said Jack, putting himself up against the wall, and lifting languidly his glass to his eye —which byplay was somewhat startling, but totally incomprehensible, to the amateur judges, who looked upon him with angry eyes.

"I must request that the proceedings may not be interrupted," said Mr Morgan ; and then everybody looked towards the open door : the sight they saw there was enough to startle the calmest spectator. Elsworthy, who was seated close by, sprang from his stool with a low resounding howl of amazement, upsetting his lowly seat, and staggering back against the wall, in the excess of his wonder and consternation. The judges themselves forgot their decorum, and crowded round upon each other to stare—old Mr Western putting his arm round the Rector's neck in his curiosity, as if they had been two boys at a peep-show. It was Miss Leonora Wentworth's erect iron-grey figure that appeared in the doorway, half leading in, half pushing before her, the unfortunate cause of all the commotion—Rosa Elsworthy herself. A change had passed upon the little girl's rosy, dewy, April beauty. Her pretty dark eyes were enlarged and anxious, and full of tears; her cheeks had paled out of their sweet colour, her red lips were pressed tightly together. Passion and shame had set their marks upon the child's forehead—lightly, it is true, but still the traces were there; but beyond all other sentiments, anxiety, restless, breathless, palpitating, had possession of Mr Wentworth's all-important witness. It was very clear that, whatever might be the opinion of her judges, Rosa's case was anything but hopeless in her own eyes. She came in drooping, shrinking, and abashed, as was natural; but her shame was secondary in Rosa's mind, even in the moment of her humiliation. She came to a dead stop when she had made a few steps into the room, and cast furtive glances at the dread tribunal, and began to cry. She was trembling with nervous eagerness, with petulance and impatience. Almost all her judges, except the Rector and Mr Proctor, had been known to Rosa from her earliest years. She was not afraid of them, nor cast down by any sense of overwhelming transgression—on the contrary, she cast an appealing look round her, which implied that they could still set everything right if they would exert themselves; and then she began to cry.

"Gentlemen, before you ask any questions," said Miss Leonora Wentworth, "I should like to explain why I am here. I came not because I approve of *her*, but because it is right that my nephew should have a respectable woman to take charge of the witness. She was brought to my house last night, and has been in my charge ever since:—and I come with her now, not because I approve of her, but because she ought to be in charge of some woman," said Miss Leonora, sitting down abruptly in the chair some one had placed for her. The chair was placed close by the spot where Rosa stood crying. Poor, pretty, forsaken child! Perhaps Miss Leonora, who sat beside her, and occupied the position of her protector, was of all the people present the only one who had not already forgiven Rosa, the only one who would have still been disposed to punish her, and did not pardon the weeping creature in her heart.

"Now that you're here, Rosa," said Dr Marjoribanks, "the only sensible thing you can do is to dry your eyes and answer the questions that have to be put to you. Nobody will harm you if you speak the truth. Don't be frightened, but dry your eyes, and let us hear what you have to say."

"Poor little thing," said old Mr Western; "of course she has done very wrong. I don't mean to defend her—but, after all, she is but a child. Poor little thing! Her mother died, you know, when she was a baby. She had nobody to tell her how to behave.—I don't mean to defend her, for she has done very wrong, poor little——"

"We are falling into mere conversation," said the Rector, severely. "Rosa Elsworthy, come to the table. The only thing you can do to make up for all the misery you have caused to your friends, is to tell the truth about everything. You are aged—how much? eighteen years?"

"Please, sir, only seventeen," said Rosa; "and oh, please, sir, I didn't mean no harm. I wouldn't never have gone, no, not a step, if he hadn't a-promised that we was to be married. Oh, please, sir——"

"Softly a little," said John Brown, interfering. "It is not you who are on your trial, Rosa

We are not going to question you about your foolishness; all that the Rector wants you to tell him is the name of the man who persuaded you to go away."

At which question Rosa cried more and more. "I don't think he meant no harm either," cried the poor little girl. "Oh, if somebody would please speak to him! We couldn't be married then, but now if anybody would take a little trouble! I told him Mr Wentworth would, if I was to ask him; but then I thought perhaps as Mr Wentworth mightn't like to be the one as married me," said Rosa, with a momentary gleam of vanity through her tears. The little simper with which the girl spoke, the coquettish looks askance at the Perpetual Curate, who stood grave and unmoved at a distance, the movement of unconscious self-deception and girlish vanity which for a moment distracted Rosa, had a great effect upon the spectators. The judges looked at each other across the table, and Dr Marjoribanks made a commentary of meditative nods upon that little exhibition. "Just so," said the Doctor; "maybe Mr Wentworth might have objected. If you tell me the man's name, *I*'ll speak to him, Rosa," said the old Scotchman, grimly.

As for the Rector, he had put down his pen altogether, and looked very much as if he were the culprit. Certainly his shame and confusion and self-disgust were greater than that of any one else in the room.

"Oh, Doctor, please don't be angry. Oh, if somebody would only speak to him!" cried poor Rosa. "Oh, please, it wasn't my fault—I haven't got no—nobody to speak for me!" At this moment she got a glimpse of her uncle's face, dark and angry, looming behind the Rector's chair. Rosa shrank back with a frightened movement, and caught fast hold of Miss Leonora's dress. "Oh, please, don't let him kill me!" cried the terrified girl. She sank down at Miss Wentworth's feet, and held tightly by her unwilling protectress. She was a frightened child, afraid of being whipped and punished; she was not an outraged woman, forsaken and miserable. Nobody knew what to do with her as she crouched down panting with fright and anxiety by Miss Leonora's side.

"We must know who this man is," said John Brown. "Look here, Rosa; if anybody is to do you good, it is necessary to know the man. Rise up and look round, and tell me if you can see him here."

After a moment's interval Rosa obeyed. She stood up trembling, resting her hand to support herself on Miss Leonora's chair—almost, she trembled so, on Miss Leonora's shoulder. Up to this moment the ignorant little creature had scarcely felt the shame of her position; she had felt only the necessity of appealing to the kindness of people who knew her—people who were powerful enough to do very nearly what they pleased in Carlingford; for it was in this light that Rosa, who knew no better, regarded the Doctor and her other judges. This time her eye passed quickly over those protectors. The tears were still hanging on her eyelashes; her childish bosom was still palpitating with sobs. Beyond the little circle of light round the table, the room was comparatively in shadow. She stood by herself, her pretty face and anxious eyes appearing over Miss Wentworth's head, her fright and her anxiety both forgotten for the moment in the sudden hope of seeing her betrayer. There was not a sound in the room to disturb the impartiality of her search. Every man kept still, as if by chance he might be the offender. Rosa's eyes, bright with anxiety, with eagerness, with a feverish hope, went searching into the shadow, gleaming harmless over the

Wentworth brothers, who were opposite. Then there was a start and a loud cry. She was not ashamed to be led before the old men, who were sorry for her, and who could protect her; but now at last the instinct of her womanhood seized upon the unfortunate creature. She had made an involuntary rush towards him when she saw him first. Then she stopped short, and looked all round her with a bewildered sudden consciousness. The blood rushed to her face, scorching and burning; she uttered a sudden cry of anguish and shame. "Oh, don't forsake me!—don't forsake me!—listen to the gentlemen!" cried poor Rosa, and fell down in a sudden agony of self-comprehension at Wodehouse's feet.

For a few minutes after there was nothing but confusion in the room. Elsworthy had been standing behind backs, with a half-fiendish look of rage and disappointment on his commonplace features. "Let them help her as likes; I washes my hands of her," he cried bitterly, when he saw her fall; and then rushed into the midst of the room, thrusting the others out of his way. The man was beside himself with mortification, with disgust, and fury, and at the same time with a savage natural affection for the creature who had baffled and disgraced him, yet still was his own. "Let alone—let alone, I tell you! There's nobody as belongs to her but me," cried Elsworthy, pushing up against the Doctor, who had lifted her from the ground. As for Wodehouse, he was standing scowling down upon the pretty figure at his feet: not that the vagabond was utterly heartless, or could look at his victim without emotion; on the contrary, he was pale with terror, thinking he had killed her, wondering in his miserable heart if they would secure him at once, and furtively watching the door to see if he had a chance of escape. When Mr Waters seized his arm, Wodehouse gave a hoarse outcry of horror. "I'll marry her—oh, Lord, I'll marry her! I never meant anything else," the wretched man cried, as he sank back again into his chair. He thought she was dead, as she lay with her upturned face on the carpet, and in his terror and remorse and cowardice his heart seemed to stop beating. If he could have had a chance of escaping, he would not have hesitated to dash the old Doctor out of his way, and rush over the body of the unhappy girl whom he thought he had murdered. But Waters held him fast; and he sank back, panting and horrified, on his seat.

"I never touched her; nobody can say I touched her," muttered the poor wretch to himself; and watched with fascinated eyes and the distinct apprehension of terror every movement and change of position, calculating how he might dart out when the window was opened—having forgotten for the moment that Jack Wentworth, as well as the companion who kept immediate watch over him, was in the room.

"She'll come to herself presently," said Dr Marjoribanks. "We'll carry her up-stairs. Yes, I know you don't approve of her, Miss Wentworth; nobody said you were to approve of her. Not that I think she's a responsible moral agent myself," said the Doctor, lifting her up in his vigorous arms; "but in the mean time she has to be brought to life. Keep out of my way, Elsworthy; you should have looked better after the little fool. If she's not accountable for her actions, *you* are," he went on with a growl, thrusting away with his vigorous shoulder the badly-hung frame of Rosa's uncle, who was no match for the Doctor. Thus the poor little girl was carried away in a kind of procession, Miss Leonora going first. "Not that I think her worth all this fuss, the vain little fool," said Miss Leonora; "she'll come to herself, no fear of her;"

but, notwithstanding her protest, the strong-minded woman led the way. When the room was cleared, the gentlemen who remained took their seats mechanically, and stared at each other. In the shame and confusion of the moment nobody could find anything to say, and the Curate was magnanimous, and did not take advantage of his triumph. The silence was broken by the Rector, who rose up solemnly from his chair to speak. Probably no one in the room had suffered so acutely as Mr Morgan; his face was crimson, his eyes suffused and angry. Frank Wentworth rose involuntarily at the same moment, expecting, he could not tell why, to be addressed, but sat down again in a little confusion when he found that the Rector had turned his eyes in a totally different direction. Mr Morgan put the lamp out of the way, that he might be able to transfix with the full glow of his angry eyes the real offender, who sat only half conscious, absorbed with his own terror, by the lawyer's side.

"Sir!" said the Rector, in a tone which, severe as his voice was by nature, nobody had ever heard from his lips before, "you have put us all in a most ridiculous and painful position to-night. I don't know whether you are capable of feeling the vileness of your own misconduct as regards the unhappy girl who has just been carried out of the room, but you certainly shall not leave the house without hearing——"

Wodehouse gave such a start at these words that Mr Morgan paused a moment. The Rector was quite unaware of the relief, the sense of safety, which he had inadvertently conveyed to the mind of the shabby rascal whom he was addressing. He was then to be allowed to leave the house? "I'll leave the d——d place to-night, by Jove!" he muttered in his beard, and immediately sat up upon his chair, and turned round with a kind of sullen vivacity to listen to the remainder of Mr Morgan's speech.

"You shall not leave this house," said the Rector, more peremptorily still, "without hearing what must be the opinion of every gentleman, of every honest man. You have been the occasion of bringing an utterly unfounded accusation against a—a young clergyman," said Mr Morgan, with a succession of gasps, "of—of the very highest character. You have, as I understand, sir, abused his hospitality, and—and done your utmost to injure him when you owed him gratitude. Not content with that, sir," continued the Rector, "you have kept your—your very existence concealed, until the moment when you could injure your sisters. You may perhaps be able to make a miserable amends for the wrong you have done to the unfortunate girl up-stairs, but you can never make amends to me, sir, for betraying me into a ridiculous position, and leading me to do—an—an absurd and—and incredible injustice—to a—to my—to Mr Frank Wentworth. Sir, you are a scoundrel!" cried Mr Morgan, breaking down abruptly in an access of sudden fury. When the Rector had recovered himself, he turned with great severity to the rest of the company: "Gentlemen, my wife will be glad to see you up-stairs," said Mr Morgan. The sound of this hospitable invitation was as if he had ordered the entire assembly to the door; but nevertheless most of the company followed him as he rose, and, without condescending to look round again, marched out of the library. The Squire rose with the rest, and took the hand of his son Frank and grasped it closely. Somehow, though he believed Frank before, Mr Wentworth was easier in his mind after the Rector's speech.

"I think I will go up-stairs and shake hands with him," said the Squire, "and you had better come too, Frank. No doubt he will expect it.

He spoke up very well at the last, and I entirely agree with the Rector," he said, looking sternly, but with a little curiosity, at the vagabond, who stood recovering himself, and ready to resume his hopeless swagger. It was well for Mr Wentworth that he left the room at once, and went cheerfully up-stairs to pay his respects to Mrs Morgan. The Squire said, "Thank God!" quietly to himself when he got out of the library. "Things are mending, surely—even Jack—even Jack," Mr Wentworth said, under his breath; and the simple gentleman said over a part of the general thanksgiving, as he went slowly, with an unusual gladness, up the stair. He might not have entered Mrs Morgan's drawing-room with such a relieved and brightened countenance had he stayed ten minutes longer in the library, and listened to the further conversation there.

CHAPTER XL.

"Now, Mr Wodehouse," said Jack Wentworth, "it appears that you and I have a word to say to each other." They had all risen when the other gentlemen followed Mr Morgan out of the room, and those who remained stood in a group surrounding the unhappy culprit, and renewing his impression of personal danger. When he heard himself thus addressed, he backed against the wall, and instinctively took one of the chairs and placed it before him. His furtive eye sought the door and the window, investigating the chances of escape. When he saw that there was none, he withdrew still a step farther back, and stood at bay.

"By Jove! I ain't going to stand all this," said Wodehouse; "as if every fellow had a right to bully me—it's more than flesh and blood can put up with. I don't care for that old fogie that's gone up-stairs; but, by Jove! I won't stand any more from men that eat my dinners, and win my money, and——"

Jack Wentworth made half a step forward with a superb smile—"My good fellow, you should never reproach a man with his good actions," he said; "but at the same time, having eaten your dinners, as you describe, I have a certain claim on your gratitude. We have had some—a—business connection—for some years. I don't say you have reason to be actually grateful for that; but, at least, it brought you now and then into the society of gentlemen. A man who robs a set of women, and leaves the poor creature he has ruined destitute, is a sort of cur we have nothing to say to," said the heir of the Wentworths, contemptuously. "We do not pretend to be saints, but we are not blackguards; that is to say," said Jack, with a perfectly calm and harmonious smile, "not in theory, nor in our own opinion. The fact accordingly is, my friend, that you must choose between *us* and those respectable meannesses of yours. By Jove! the fellow ought to have been a shopkeeper, and as honest as—Diogenes," said Jack. He stood looking at his wretched associate with the overwhelming impertinence of a perfectly well-bred man, no way concealing the contemptuous inspection with which his cool eyes travelled over the disconcerted figure from top to toe, seeing and exaggerating all its tremors and clumsy guiltiness. The chances are, had Jack Wentworth been in Wodehouse's place, he would have been master of the position as much as now. He was not shocked nor indignant like his brothers. He was simply contemptuous, disdainful, not so much of the wickedness as of the clumsy and shabby fashion in which it had been accomplished. As for the offender, who had been defiant in his sulky fashion up to this moment, his courage oozed out at his finger-ends under Jack Wentworth's eye.

"I am my own master," he stammered, "now-adays. I ain't to be dictated to—and I shan't be, by Jove! As for Jack Wentworth, he's well known to be neither more nor less——"

"Than what, Mr Wodehouse?" said the serene and splendid Jack. "Don't interest yourself on my account, Frank. This is my business at present. If you have any prayer-meetings in hand, we can spare you—and don't forget our respectable friend in your supplications. Favour us with your definition of Jack

Wentworth, Mr Wodehouse. He is neither more nor less——?"

"By Jove! I ain't going to stand it," cried Wodehouse; "if a fellow's to be driven mad, and insulted, and have his money won from him, and made game of—not to say tossed about as I've been among 'em, and made a drudge of, and set to do the dirty work," said the unfortunate subordinate, with a touch of pathos in his hoarse voice;—"I don't mean to say I've been what I ought; but, by Jove! to be put upon as I've been, and knocked about; and at the last they haven't the pluck to stand by a fellow, by Jove!" muttered Mr Wodehouse's unlucky heir. What further exasperation his smiling superior intended to heap upon him, nobody could tell; for just as Jack Wentworth was about to speak, and just as Wodehouse had again faced towards him, half-cowed, half-resisting, Gerald, who had been looking on in silence, came forward out of the shadow. He had seen all and heard all, from that moral death-bed of his, where no personal cares could again disturb him; and though he had resigned his office, he could not belie his nature. He came in by instinct to cherish the dawn of compunction which appeared, as he thought, in the sinner's words.

"The best thing that can happen to you," said Gerald, at the sound of whose voice everybody started, "is to find out that the wages of sin are bitter. Don't expect any sympathy or consolation from those who have helped you to do wrong. My brother tries to induce you to do a right act from an unworthy motive. He says your former associates will not acknowledge you. My advice to you is to forsake your former associates. My brother," said Gerald, turning aside to look at him, "would do himself honour if he forsook them also—but for you, here is your opportunity. You have no temptation of poverty now. Take the first step, and forsake them. I have no motive in advising you—except, indeed, that I am Jack Wentworth's brother. He and you are different," said Gerald, involuntarily glancing from one to the other. "And at present you have the means of escape. Go now and leave them," said the man who was a priest by nature. The light returned to his eye while he spoke; he was no longer passive, contemplating his own moral death; his natural office had come back to him unawares. He stretched his arm towards the door, thinking of nothing but the escape of the sinner. "Go," said Gerald. "Refuse their approbation; shun their society. For Christ's sake, and not for theirs, make amends to those you have wronged. Jack, I command you to let him go."

Jack, who had been startled at first, had recovered himself long before his brother ceased to speak. "Let him go, by all means," he said, and stood superbly indifferent by Gerald's side, whistling under his breath a tripping lively air. "No occasion for solemnity. The sooner he goes the better," said Jack. "In short, I see no reason why any of us should stay, now the business is accomplished. I wonder would his reverence ever forgive me if I lighted my cigar?" He took out his case as he spoke, and began to look over its contents. There was one in the room, however, who was better acquainted with the indications of Jack Wentworth's face than either of his brothers. This unfortunate, who was hanging in an agony of uncertainty over the chair he had placed before him, watched every movement of his leader's face with the anxious gaze of a lover, hoping to see a little corresponding anxiety in it, but watched in vain. Wodehouse had been going through a fever of doubt and divided impulses. The shabby fellow was open to good impressions, though he was not much in the way of practising them; and Gerald's address, which, in the first place, filled him with awe, moved him afterwards with passing thrills of compunction, mingled with a kind of delight at the idea of getting free. When his admonitor said "Go," Wodehouse made a step towards the door, and for an instant felt the exhilaration of enfranchisement. But the next moment his eye sought Jack Wentworth's face, which was so superbly careless, so indifferent to him and his intentions, and the vagabond's soul succumbed with a canine fidelity to his master. Had Jack shown any interest, any excitement in the matter, his sway might have been doubtful; but in proportion to the sense of his own insignificance and unimportance Wodehouse's allegiance confirmed itself. He looked wistfully towards the hero of his imagination, as that skilful personage selected his cigar. He would rather have been kicked again than left alone, and left to himself. After all, it was very true what Jack Wentworth said. They might be a bad lot, but they were gentlemen (according to Wodehouse's understanding of the word) with whom he had been associated; and beatific visions of peers and baronets and honourables, amongst whom his own shabby person had figured, without feeling much below the common level, crossed his mind with all the sweetness which belongs to a past state of affairs. Yet it was still in his power to recall these vanishing glories. Now that he was rich, and could "cut a figure" among the objects of his admiration, was that brilliant world to be closed upon him for ever by his own obstinacy? As these thoughts rushed through his mind, little Rosa's beauty and natural grace came suddenly to his recollection. Nobody need know how he had got his pretty wife, and a pretty wife she would be— a creature whom nobody could help admiring. Wodehouse looked wistfully at Jack Wentworth, who took no notice of him as he chose his cigar. Jack was not only the ideal of the clumsier rogue, but he was the doorkeeper of that paradise of disreputable nobles and ruined gentlemen which was Wodehouse's idea of good society; and from all this was he about to be banished? Jack Wentworth selected his cigar with as much care as if his happiness depended on it, and took no notice of the stealthy glances thrown at him. "I'll get a light in the hall," said Jack; "good evening to you," and he was actually going away.

"Look here," said Wodehouse, hastily, in his beard; "I ain't a man to forsake old friends. If Jack Wentworth does not mean anything unreasonable, or against a fellow's honour——. Hold your tongue, Waters; by Jove! I know my friends. I know you would never have been one of them but for Jack Wentworth. He's not the common sort, I can tell you. He's the greatest swell going, by Jove!" cried Jack's admiring follower, "and through thick and thin he's stood by me. I ain't going to forsake him now—that is, if he don't want anything that goes against a fellow's honour," said the repentant prodigal, again sinking the voice which he had raised for a moment. As he spoke he looked more wistfully than ever towards his leader, who said "Pshaw!" with an impatient gesture, and put back his cigar.

"This room is too hot for anything," said Jack; "but don't open the window, I entreat of you. I hate to assist at the suicide of a set of insane insects. For heaven's sake, Frank, mind what you're doing. As for Mr Wodehouse's remark," said Jack, lightly, "I trust I never could suggest anything which would wound his keen sense of honour. I advise you to marry and settle, as I am in the habit of advising young men; and if I were to add that it would be seemly to make some provision for your sisters——"

"Stop there!" said the Curate, who had taken no part in the scene up to this moment. He had stood behind rather contemptuously, determined to have nothing to do with his ungrateful and ungenerous protégé. But now an unreasonable impulse forced him into the discussion. "The less that is said on that part of the subject the better," he said, with some natural heat. "I object to the mixing up of names which—which no one here has any right to bandy about——"

"That is very true," said Mr Proctor; "but still they have their rights," the late Rector added after a pause. "We have no right to stand in the way of their—their interest, you know." It occurred to Mr Proctor, indeed, that the suggestion was on the whole a sensible one. "Even if they were to—to marry, you know, they might still be left unprovided for," said the late Rector. "I think it is quite just that some provision should be made for that."

And then there was a pause. Frank Wentworth was sufficiently aware after his first start of indignation that he had no right to interfere, as Mr Proctor said, between the Miss Wodehouses and their interest. He had no means of providing for them, of setting them above the chances of fortune. He reflected bitterly that it was not in his power to offer a home to Lucy, and through her to her sister. What he had to do was to stand by silently, to suffer other people to discuss what was to be done for the woman whom he loved, and whose name was sacred to him. This was a stretch of patience of which he was not capable. "I can only say again," said the Curate, "that I think this discussion has gone far enough. Whatever matters of business there may be that require arrangement had better be settled between Mr Brown and Mr Waters. So far as private feeling goes——"

"Never fear, I'll manage it," said Jack Wentworth, "as well as a dozen lawyers. Private feeling has nothing to do with it. Have a cigar, Wodehouse? We'll talk it over as we walk home," said the condescending potentate. These words dispersed the assembly, which no longer had any object. As Jack Wentworth sauntered out, his faithful follower pressed through the others to join him. Wodehouse was himself again. He gave a sulky nod to the Curate, and said, "Good-night, parson; I don't owe much to you," and hastened out close upon the heels of his patron and leader. All the authorities of Carlingford, the virtuous people who conferred station and respectability by a look, sank into utter insignificance in presence of Jack. His admiring follower went after him with a swell of pride. He was a poor enough rogue himself, hustled and abused by everybody, an unsuccessful and shabby vagabond, notwithstanding his new fortune; but Jack was the glorified impersonation of cleverness and wickedness and triumph to Wodehouse. He grew insolent when he was permitted to put his arm through that of his hero, and went off with him trying to copy, in swagger and insolence, his careless step and well-bred ease. Perhaps Jack Wentworth felt a little ashamed of himself as he emerged from the gate of the Rectory with his shabby and disreputable companion. He shrugged his shoulders slightly as he looked back and saw Gerald and Frank coming slowly out together. "Coraggio!" said Jack to himself, "it is I who am the true philanthropist. Let us do evil that good may come." Notwithstanding, he was very thankful not to be seen by his father, who had wished to consult him as a man of the world, and had shown certain yearnings towards him, which, to Jack's infinite surprise, awakened responsive feelings in his own unaccustomed bosom. He was half ashamed of this secret movement of natural affection, which, certainly, nobody else suspected; but it was with a sensation of relief that he closed the Rectory gate behind him, without having encountered the keen, inquiring, suspicious glances of the Squire. The others dispersed according to their pleasure —Mr Waters joining the party up-stairs, while Mr Proctor followed Jack Wentworth and Wodehouse to the door with naïve natural curiosity. When the excellent man recollected that he was listening to private conversation, and met Wodehouse's look of sulky insolence, he turned back again, much fluttered and disturbed. He had an interest in the matter, though the two in whose hands it now lay were the last whom he would have chosen as confidants; and to do him justice, he was thinking of Lucy only in his desire to hear what they decided upon. "Something might happen to me," he said to himself; "and, even if all was well, she would be happier not to be wholly dependent upon her sister;" with which self-exculpatory reflection, Mr Proctor slowly followed the others into the drawing-room. Gerald and Frank, who were neither of them disposed for society, went away together. They had enough to think of, without much need of conversation, and they had walked half-way down Grange Lane before either spoke. Then it was Frank who broke the silence abruptly with a question which had nothing to do with the business in which they had been engaged.

"And what do you mean to do?" said Frank, suddenly. It was just as they came in sight of the graceful spire of St Roque's; and perhaps it was the sight of his own church which roused the Perpetual Curate to think of the henceforth aimless life of his brother. "I don't understand how you are to give up your work. To-night even——"

"I did not forget myself," said Gerald; "every man who can distinguish good from evil has a right to advise his fellow-creature. I have not given up that common privilege —don't hope it, Frank," said the martyr, with a momentary smile.

"If I could but understand why it is that you make this terrible sacrifice!" said the Curate —"No, I don't want to argue—of course, you are convinced. I can understand the wish that our unfortunate division had never taken place; but I can't understand the sacrifice of a man's life and work. Nothing is perfect in this world; but at least to do something in it—to be good for something—and with your faculties, Gerald!" cried the admiring and regretful brother. "Can abstract right in an institution, if that is what you aim at, be worth the sacrifice of your existence—your power of influencing your fellow-creatures?" This Mr Wentworth said, being specially moved by the circumstances in which he found himself—for, under any other conditions, such sentiments would have produced the warmest opposition in his Anglican bosom. But he was so far sympathetic that he could be tolerant to his brother who had gone to Rome.

"I know what you mean," said Gerald; "it is the prevailing theory in England that all human institutions are imperfect. My dear Frank, I want a Church which is not a human institution. In England it seems to be the rule of faith that every man may believe as he pleases. There is no authority either to decide or to punish. If you can foresee what that may lead us to, I cannot. I take refuge in the true Church, where alone there is certainty

—where," said the convert, with a heightened colour and a long-drawn breath, "there is authority clear and decisive. In England you believe what you will, and the result will be one that I at least fear to contemplate; in Rome we believe what—we must," said Gerald. He said the words slowly, bowing his head more than once with determined submission, as if bending under the yoke. "Frank, it is salvation!" said the new Catholic, with the emphasis of a despairing hope. And for the first time Frank Wentworth perceived what it was which had driven his brother to Rome.

"I understand you now," said the Perpetual Curate; "it is because there is no room for our conflicting doctrines and latitude of belief. Instead of a Church happily so far imperfect, that a man can put his life to the best account in it, without absolutely delivering up his intellect to a set of doctrines, you seek a perfect Church, in which, for a symmetrical system of doctrine, you lose the use of your existence!" Mr Wentworth uttered this opinion with all the more vehemence, that it was in direct opposition to his own habitual ideas; but even his veneration for his "Mother" yielded for the moment to his strong sense of his brother's mistake.

"It is a hard thing to say," said Gerald, "but it is true. If you but knew the consolation, after years of struggling among the problems of faith, to find one's self at last upon a rock of authority, of certainty—one holds in one's hand at last the interpretation of the enigma," said Gerald. He looked up to the sky as he spoke, and breathed into the serene air a wistful lingering sigh. If it was certainty that echoed in that breath of unsatisfied nature, the sound was sadly out of concord with the sentiment. His soul, notwithstanding that expression of serenity, was still as wistful as the night.

"Have you the interpretation?" said his brother; and Frank, too, looked up into the pure sky above, with its stars which stretched over them serene and silent, arching over the town that lay behind, and of which nobody knew better than he the human mysteries and wonderful unanswerable questions. The heart of the Curate ached to think how many problems lay in the darkness, over which that sky stretched silent, making no sign. There were the sorrowful of the earth, enduring their afflictions, lifting up pitiful hands, demanding of God in their bereavements and in their miseries the reason why. There were all the inequalities of life, side by side, evermore echoing dumbly the same awful question; and over all shone the calm sky which gave no answer. "Have you the interpretation?" he said. "Perhaps you can reconcile freewill and predestination—the need of a universal atonement and the existence of individual virtue? But these are not to me the most difficult questions. Can your Church explain why one man is happy and another miserable?—why one has everything and abounds, and the other loses all that is most precious in life? My sister Mary, for example," said the Curate, "she seems to bear the cross for our family. Her children die and yours live. Can you explain to her why? I have heard her cry out to God to know the reason, and He made no answer. Tell me, have you the interpretation?" cried the young man, on whom the hardness of his own position was pressing at the moment. They went on together in silence for a few minutes, without any attempt on Gerald's part to answer. "You accept the explanation of the Church in respect to doctrines," said the Curate, after that pause, "and consent that her authority is sufficient, and that your perplexity is over—that is well enough, so far as it goes: but outside lies a world in which every event is an enigma, where nothing that comes offers any explanation of itself; where God does not show Himself always kind, but by times awful, terrible—a God who smites and does not spare. It is easy to make a harmonious balance of doctrine; but where is the interpretation of life?" The young priest looked back on his memory, and recalled, as if they had been in a book, the daily problems with which he was so well acquainted. As for Gerald, he bowed his head a little, with a kind of reverence, as if he had been bowing before the shrine of a saint.

"I have had a happy life," said the elder brother. "I have not been driven to ask such questions for myself. To these the Church has but one advice to offer: Trust God."

"We say so in England," said Frank Wentworth; "it is the grand scope of our teaching. Trust God. He will not explain Himself, nor can we attempt it. When it is certain that I must be content with this answer for all the sorrows of life, I am content to take my doctrines on the same terms," said the Perpetual Curate;—and by this time they had come to Miss Wentworth's door. After all, perhaps it was not Gerald, except so far as he was carried by a wonderful force of human sympathy and purity of soul, who was the predestined priest of the family. As he went up to his own room, a momentary spasm of doubt came upon the new convert—whether, perhaps, he was making a sacrifice of his life for a mistake. He hushed the thought forcibly as it rose; such impulses were no longer to be listened to. The same authority which made faith certain, decided every doubt to be sin.

CHAPTER XLI.

NEXT morning the Curate got up with anticipations which were far from cheerful, and a weary sense of the monotony and dulness of life. He had won his little battle, it was true; but the very victory had removed that excitement which answered in the absence of happier stimulants to keep up his heart and courage. After a struggle like that in which he had been engaged, it was hard to come again into the peaceable routine without any particular hope to enliven or happiness to cheer it, which was all he had at present to look for in his life; and it was harder still to feel the necessity of being silent, of standing apart from Lucy in her need, of shutting up in his own heart the longing he had towards her, and refraining himself from the desperate thought of uniting his genteel beggary to hers. That was the one thing which must not be thought of, and he subdued himself with an impatient sigh, and could not but wonder, as he went down-stairs, whether, if Gerald had been less smoothly guided through the perplexing paths of life, he would have found time for all the difficulties which had driven him to take refuge in Rome. It was with this sense of hopeless restraint and incapacity, which is perhaps of all sensations the most humbling, that he went down-stairs, and found lying on his breakfast table, the first thing that met his eye, the note which Lucy Wodehouse had written to him on the previous night. As he read it, the earth somehow turned to the sun; the dubious light brightened in the skies. Unawares, he had been wondering never to receive any token of sympathy, any word of encouragement, from those for whom he had made so many exertions. When he had read Lucy's letter, the aspect of affairs changed considerably. To be sure, nothing that she had said or could say made any difference in the facts of the case; but the Curate was young, and still liable to those changes of atmosphere which do more for an imaginative mind than real revolutions. He read the letter several times over as he lingered through his breakfast, making on the whole an agreeable meal, and finding himself repossessed of his ordinary healthful appetite. He even canvassed the signature as much in reading as Lucy had done in writing it—balancing in his mind the maidenly "truly yours" of that subscription with as many ingenious renderings of its possible meaning, as if Lucy's letter had been articles of faith. "Truly mine," he said to himself, with a smile; which indeed meant all a lover could require; and then paused, as if he had been Dr Lushington or Lord Westbury, to inquire into the real force of the phrase. For after all, it is not only when signing the Articles that the bond and pledge of subscription means more than is intended. When Mr Wentworth was able to tear himself from the agreeable casuistry of this self-discussion, he got up in much better spirits to go about his daily business. First of all, he had to see his father, and ascertain what were the Squire's intentions, and how long he meant to stay in Carlingford; and then—— It occurred to the Perpetual Curate that after that, politeness demanded that he should call on the Miss Wodehouses, who had, or at least one of them, expressed so frankly their confidence in him. He could not but call to thank her, to inquire into their plans, perhaps to back aunt Leonora's invitation, which he was aware had been gratefully declined. With these ideas in his mind he went down-stairs, after brushing his hat very carefully and casting one solicitous glance in the mirror as he passed—which presented to him a very creditable reflection, an eidolon in perfect clerical apparel, without any rusty suggestions of a Perpetual Curacy. Yet a Perpetual Curacy it was which was his sole benefice or hope in his present circumstances, for he knew very well that, were all other objections at an end, neither Skelmersdale nor Wentworth could be kept open for him; and that beyond these two he had not a hope of advancement—and at the same time he was pledged to remain in Carlingford. All this, however, though discouraging enough, did not succeed in discouraging Mr Wentworth after he had read Lucy's letter. He went down-stairs so lightly that Mrs Hadwin, who was waiting in the parlour in her best cap, to ask if he would pardon her for making such a mistake, did not hear him pass, and sat waiting for an hour, forgetting, or rather neglecting to give any response, when the butcher came for orders—which was an unprecedented accident. Mr Wentworth went cheerfully up Grange Lane, meeting, by a singular chance, ever so many people, who stopped to shake hands with him, or at least bowed their good wishes and friendly acknowledgments. He smiled in himself at these evidences of popular penitence, but was not the less pleased to find himself reinstated in his place in the affections and respect of Carlingford. "After all, it was not an unnatural mistake," he said to himself, and smiled benignly upon the excellent people who had found out the error of their own ways. Carlingford, indeed, seemed altogether in a more cheerful state than usual, and Mr Wentworth could not but think that the community in general was glad to find that it had been deceived, and so went upon his way, pleasing himself with those maxims about the ultimate prevalence of justice and truth, which make it apparent that goodness is always victorious, and wickedness punished, in the end. Somehow even a popular fallacy has an aspect of truth when it suits one's own case. The Perpetual Curate went through his aunt's garden with a conscious smile, feeling once more master of himself and his concerns. There was, to tell the truth, even a slight shade of self-content and approbation upon his handsome countenance. In the present changed state of public opinion and private feeling, he began to take some pleasure in his sacrifice. To be sure, a Perpetual Curate could not marry; but perhaps Lucy—in short, there was no telling what might happen; and it was accordingly with that delicious sense of goodness which generally attends an act of self-sacrifice, mingled with an equally delicious feeling that the act, when accomplished, might turn out no such great sacrifice after all—which it is to be feared is the most usual way in which the sacrifices of youth are made—that the Curate walked into the hall, passing his aunt Dora's toy terrier without that violent inclination to give it a whack with his cane in passing, which was his usual state of feeling. To tell the truth, Lucy's letter had made him at peace with all the world.

When, however, he entered the dining-room, where the family were still at breakfast, Frank's serenity was unexpectedly disturbed. The first thing that met his eye was his aunt Leonora, towering over her tea-urn at the upper end of the table, holding in her hand a letter which she had just opened. The envelope had fallen in the midst of the immaculate breakfast "things," and indeed lay, with its broad black edge on the top of the snow-white lumps, in Miss Leonora's own sugar-basin; and the news had been sufficiently interesting to suspend the operations of tea-making, and to bring the strong-minded woman to her feet. The first words which were audible to Frank revealed to him the nature of the intelligence which had produced such startling effects.

"He was always a contradictory man," said Miss Leonora; "since the first hour he was in Skelmersdale, he has made a practice of doing things at the wrong time. I don't mean to reproach the poor man now he's gone; but when he has been so long of going, what good could it do him to choose this particular moment, for no other reason that I can see, except that it was specially uncomfortable to us? What my brother has just been saying makes it all the worse," said Miss Leonora, with a look of annoyance. She had turned her head away from the door, which was at the side of the room, and had not perceived the entrance of the Curate. "As long as we could imagine that Frank was to succeed to the Rectory, the thing looked comparatively easy. I beg your pardon, Gerald. Of course, you know how grieved I am—in short, that we all feel the deepest distress and vexation; but, to be sure, since you have given it up, somebody must succeed you—there can be no doubt of that."

"Not the least, my dear aunt," said Gerald.

"I am glad you grant so much. It is well to be sure of something," said the incisive and peremptory speaker. "It would have been a painful thing for us at any time to place another person in Skelmersdale while Frank was unprovided for; but, of course," said Miss Leonora, sitting down suddenly, "nobody who knows me could suppose for a minute that I would let my feelings stand in the way of my public duty. Still it is very awkward just at this moment, when Frank, on the whole, has been behaving very properly, and one can't help so far approving of him——"

"I am much obliged to you, aunt Leonora," said the Curate.

"Oh, you are there, Frank," said his sensible aunt; and strong-minded though she was, a slight shade of additional colour appeared for a moment on Miss Leonora's face. She paused a little, evidently diverted from the line of discourse which she had contemplated, and wavered liked a vessel disturbed in its course. "The fact is, I have just had a letter announcing Mr Shirley's death," she continued, facing round towards her nephew, and setting off abruptly, in face of all consequences, on the new tack.

"I am very sorry," said Frank Wentworth; "though I have an old grudge at him on account of his long sermons; but as you have expected it for a year or two, I can't imagine your grief to be overwhelming," said the Curate, with a touch of natural impertinence to be expected under the circumstances. Skelmersdale had been so long thought interesting to him, that now, when it was not in the least interesting, he got impatient of the name.

"I quite agree with you, Frank," said Miss Wentworth. Aunt Cecilia had not been able for a long time to agree with anybody. She had been, on the contrary, shaking her head and shedding a few gentle tears over Gerald's silent submission and Louisa's noisy lamentations. Everything was somehow going wrong; and she who had no power to mend, at least could not assent, and broke through her old use and wont to shake her head, which was a thing very alarming to the family. The entire party was moved by a sensation of pleasure to hear

Miss Cecilia say, "I quite agree with you, Frank."

"You are looking better this morning, my dear aunt," said Gerald. They had a great respect for each other these two; but when Miss Cecilia turned to hear what her elder nephew was saying, her face lost the momentary look of approval it had worn, and she again, though very softly, almost imperceptibly, began to shake her head.

"We were not asking for your sympathy," said Miss Leonora, sharply. "Don't talk like a saucy boy. We were talking of our own embarrassment. There is a very excellent young man, the curate of the parish, whom Julia Trench is to be married to. By the way, of course, this must put it off; but I was about to say, when you interrupted me, that to give it away from you at this moment, just as you had been doing well—doing—your duty," said Miss Leonora, with unusual hesitation, "was certainly very uncomfortable, to say the least, to us."

"Don't let that have the slightest influence on you, I beg," cried the Perpetual Curate, with all the pride of his years. "I hope I have been doing my duty all along," the young man added, more softly, a moment after; upon which the Squire gave a little nod, partly of satisfaction and encouragement to his son—partly of remonstrance and protest to his sister.

"Yes, I suppose so — with the flowers at Easter, for example," said Miss Leonora, with a slight sneer. "I consider that I have stood by you through all this business, Frank—but, of course, in so important a matter as a cure of souls, neither relationship nor, to a certain extent, approval," said Miss Leonora, with again some hesitation, "can be allowed to stand against public duty. We have the responsibility of providing a good gospel minister——"

"I beg your pardon for interrupting you, Leonora," said the Squire, "but I can't help thinking that you make a mistake. I think it's a man's bounden duty, when there is a living in the family, to educate one of his sons for it. In my opinion, it's one of the duties of property. You have no right to live off your estate, and spend your money elsewhere; and no more have you any right to give less than—than your own flesh and blood to the people you have the charge of. You've got the charge of them to — to a certain extent — soul and body, sir," said the Squire, growing warm, as he put down his 'Times,' and forgetting that he addressed a lady. "I'd never have any peace of mind if I filled up a family living with a stranger — unless, of course," Mr Wentworth added in a parenthesis—an unlikely sort of contingency which had not occurred to him at first—"you should happen to have no second son.—The eldest the squire, the second the rector. That's my idea, Leonora, of Church and State."

Miss Leonora smiled a little at her brother's semi-feudal, semi-pagan ideas. "I have long known that we were not of the same way of thinking," said the strong-minded aunt, who, though cleverer than her brother, was too wise in her own conceit to perceive at the first glance the noble, simple conception of his own duties and position, which was implied in the honest gentleman's words. "Your second son might be either a fool or a knave, or even, although neither, might be quite unfit to be intrusted with the eternal interests of his fellow-creatures. In my opinion, the duty of choosing a clergyman is one not to be exercised without the gravest deliberation. A conscientious man would make his selection dependent, at least, upon the character of his second son—if he had one. We, however——"

"But then his character is *so* satisfactory, Leonora," cried Miss Dora, feeling emboldened by the shadow of visitors under whose shield she could always retire. "Everybody knows what a good clergyman he is—I am sure it would be like a new world in Skelmersdale if you were there, Frank, my dear—and preaches such beautiful sermons!" said the unlucky little woman, upon whom her sister immediately descended, swift and sudden, like a storm at sea.

"We are generally perfectly of accord in our conclusions," said Miss Leonora; "as for Dora, she comes to the same end by a roundabout way. After what my brother has been saying——"

"Yes," said the Squire, with uncomfortable looks, "I was saying to your aunt, Frank, what I said to you about poor Mary. Since Gerald *will* go, and since you don't want to come, the best thing to do would be to have Huxtable. He's a very good fellow on the whole, and it might cheer her up, poor soul, to be near her sisters. Life has been hard work to her, poor girl—very hard work, sir," said the Squire, with a sigh. The idea was troublesome and uncomfortable, and always disturbed his mind when it occurred to him. It was indeed a secret humiliation to the Squire, that his eldest daughter possessed so little the characteristic health and prosperity of the Wentworths. He was very sorry for her, but yet half angry and half ashamed, as if she could have helped it; but, however, he had been obliged to admit, in his private deliberations on the subject, that, failing Frank, Mary's husband had the next best right to Wentworth Rectory—an arrangement of which Miss Leonora did not approve.

"I was about to say that we have no second son," she said, taking up the thread of her discourse where it had been interrupted. "Our duty is solely towards the Christian people. I do not pretend to be infallible," said Miss Leonora, with a meek air of self-contradiction; "but I should be a very poor creature indeed, if, at my age, I did not know what I believed, and was not perfectly convinced that I am right. Consequently (though, I repeat, Mr Shirley has chosen the most inconvenient moment possible for dying), it can't be expected of me that I should appoint my nephew, whose opinions in most points are exactly the opposite of mine."

"I wish, at least, you would believe what I say," interrupted the Curate, impatiently.

"There might have been some sense in all this three months ago; but if Skelmersdale were the highroad to everything desirable in the Church, you are all quite aware that I could not accept it. Stop, Gerald; I am not so disinterested as you think," said Frank; "if I left Carlingford now, people would remember against me that my character had been called in question here. I can remain a Perpetual Curate," said the young man, with a smile, "but I can't tolerate any shadow upon my honour. I am sorry I came in at such an awkward moment. Good morning, aunt Leonora. I hope Julia Trench, when she has the Rectory, will always keep of your way of thinking. She used to incline a little to mine," he said, mischievously, as he went away.

"Come back, Frank, presently," said the Squire, whose attention had been distracted from his 'Times.' Mr Wentworth began to be tired of such a succession of exciting discussions. He thought if he had Frank quietly to himself he could settle matters much more agreeably; but the 'Times' was certainly an accompaniment more tranquillising so far as a comfortable meal was concerned.

"He can't come back presently," said aunt

Leonora. "You speak as if he had nothing to do; when, on the contrary, he has everything to do—that is worth doing," said that contradictory authority. "Come back to lunch, Frank; and I wish you would eat your breakfast, Dora, and not stare at me."

Miss Dora had come down to breakfast as an invalid, in a pretty little cap, with a shawl over her dressing-gown. She had not yet got over her adventure and the excitement of Rosa's capture. That unusual accident, and all the applauses of her courage which had been addressed to her since, had roused the timid woman. She did not withdraw her eyes from her sister, though commanded to do so; on the contrary, her look grew more and more emphatic. She meant to have made a solemn address, throwing off Leonora's yoke, and declaring her intention, in this grave crisis of her nephew's fortunes, of acting for herself; but her feelings were too much for Miss Dora. The tears came creeping to the corners of her eyes, and she could not keep them back; and her attempt at dignity broke down. "I am never consulted," she said, with a gasp. "I don't mean to pretend to know better than Leonora; but—but I think it is very hard that Frank should be disappointed about Skelmersdale. You may call me as foolish as you please," said Miss Dora, with rising tears, "I know everybody will say it is my fault; but I must say I think it is very hard that Frank should be disappointed. He was always brought up for it, as everybody knows; and to disappoint him, who is so good and so nice, for a fat young man, buttered all over like—like—a pudding-basin," cried poor Miss Dora, severely adhering to the unity of her desperate metaphor. "I don't know what Julia Trench can be thinking of; I—I don't know what Leonora means."

"I am of the same way of thinking," said aunt Cecilia, setting down, with a little gentle emphasis, her cup of tea.

Here was rebellion, open and uncompromised. Miss Leonora was so much taken by surprise, that she lifted the tea-urn out of the way, and stared at her interlocutors with genuine amazement. But she proved herself, as usual, equal to the occasion.

"It's unfortunate that we never see eye to eye just at once," she said, with a look which expressed more distinctly than words could have done the preliminary flourish of his whip, by means of which a skilful charioteer gets his team under hand without touching them; "but it is very lucky that we always come to agree in the end," she added, more significantly still. It was well to crush insubordination in the bud. Not that she did not share the sentiment of her sisters; but then they were guided like ordinary women by their feelings, whereas Miss Leonora had the rights of property before her, and the approval of Exeter Hall.

"And he wants to marry, poor dear boy," said Miss Dora, pale with fright, yet persevering; "and she is a dear good girl—the very person for a clergyman's wife; and what is he to do if he is always to be Curate of St Roque's? You may say it is my fault, but I cannot help it. He always used to come to me in all his little troubles; and when he wants anything very particular, he knows there is nothing I would not do for him," sobbed the proud aunt, who could not help recollecting how much use she had been to Frank. She wiped her eyes at the thought, and held up her head with a thrill of pride and satisfaction. Nobody could blame her in that particular at least. "He knew he had only to tell me what he wanted," said Miss Dora, swelling out her innocent plumes. Jack, who was sitting opposite, and who had been listening with admiration, thought it time to come in on his own part.

"I hope you don't mean to forsake *me*, aunt Dora," he said. "If a poor fellow cannot have faith in his aunt, whom can he have faith in? I thought it was too good to last," said the neglected prodigal. "You have left the poor sheep in the wilderness and gone back to the ninety-and-nine righteous men who need no repentance." He put up his handkerchief to his eyes as he spoke, and so far forgot himself as to look with laughter in his face at his brother Gerald. As for the Squire, he was startled to hear his eldest son quoting Scripture, and laid aside his paper once more to know what it meant.

"I am sure I beg your pardon, Jack," said aunt Dora, suddenly stopping short, and feeling guilty. "I never meant to neglect you. Poor dear boy, he never was properly tried with female society and the comforts of home; but then you were dining out that night," said the simple woman, eagerly. "I should have stayed with you, Jack, *of course*, had you been at home."

From this little scene Miss Leonora turned away hastily, with an exclamation of impatience. She made an abrupt end of her tea-making, and went off to her little business-room with a grim smile upon her iron-grey countenance. She too had been taken in a little by Jack's pleasant farce of the Sinner Repentant; and it occurred to her to feel a little ashamed of herself as she went up-stairs. After all, the ninety-and-nine just men of Jack's irreverent quotation were worth considering now and then; and Miss Leonora could not but think with a little humiliation of the contrast between her nephew Frank and the comfortable young Curate who was going to marry Julia Trench. He *was* fat, it could not be denied; and she remembered his chubby looks, and his sermons about self-denial and mortification of the flesh, much as a pious Catholic might think of the Lenten oratory of a fat friar. But then he was perfectly sound in his doctrines, and it was undeniable that the people liked him, and that the appointment was one which even a Scotch ecclesiastical community full of popular rights could scarcely have objected to. According to her own principles, the strong-minded woman could not do otherwise. She threw herself into her arm-chair with unnecessary force, and read over the letter which Miss Trench herself had written. "It is difficult to think of any consolation in such a bereavement," wrote Mr Shirley's niece; "but still it is a little comfort to feel that I can throw myself on your sympathy, my dear and kind friend." "Little calculating thing!" Miss Leonora said to herself as she threw down the mournful epistle; and then she could not help thinking again of Frank. To be sure, he was not of her way of thinking; but when she remembered the "investigation" and its result, and the secret romance involved in it, her Wentworth blood sent a thrill of pride and pleasure through her veins. Miss Leonora, though she was strong-minded, was still woman enough to perceive her nephew's motives in his benevolence to Wodehouse; but these motives, which were strong enough to make him endure so much annoyance, were not strong enough to tempt him from Carlingford and his Perpetual Curacy, where his honour and reputation, in the face of love and ambition, demanded that he should remain. "It would be a pity to balk him in his self-sacrifice," she said to herself, with again a somewhat grim smile, and a comparison not much to the advantage of Julia Trench and *her* curate. She shut herself up among her papers till luncheon, and only emerged with a stormy front when that meal was on the table; during the progress of which she snubbed everybody who ventured to speak to her, and spoke to her nephew Frank as if he might have been suspected of designs upon the plate-chest. Such were the unpleasant consequences of the struggle between duty and inclination in the bosom of Miss Leonora; and, save for other unforeseen events which decided the matter for her, it is not by any means so certain as, judging from her character, it ought to have been, that duty would have won the day.

CHAPTER XLII.

Frank Wentworth once more went up Grange Lane, a thoughtful and a sober man. Exhilaration comes but by moments in the happiest of lives—and already he began to remember how very little he had to be elated about, and how entirely things remained as before. Even Lucy; her letter very probably might be only an effusion of friendship; and at all events, what could he say to her—what did he dare in honour say? And then his mind went off to think of the two rectories, between which he had fallen as between two stools: though he had made up his mind to accept neither, he did not the less feel a certain mortification in seeing that his relations on both sides were so willing to bestow their gifts elsewhere. He could not tolerate the idea of succeeding Gerald in his own person, but still he found it very disagreeable to consent to the thought that Huxtable should replace him—Huxtable, who was a good fellow enough, but of whom Frank Wentworth thought, as men generally think of their brothers-in-law, with a half-impatient, half-contemptuous wonder what Mary could ever have seen in so commonplace a man. To think of him as rector of Wentworth inwardly chafed the spirit of the Perpetual Curate. As he was going along, absorbed in his own thoughts, he did not perceive how his approach was watched for from the other side of the way by Elsworthy, who stood with his bundle of newspapers under his arm and his hat in his hand, watching for "his clergyman" with submission and apology on the surface, and hidden rancour underneath. Elsworthy was not penitent; he was furious and disappointed. His mistake and its consequences were wholly humiliating, and had not in them a single saving feature to atone for the wounds of his self-esteem. The Curate had not only baffled and beaten him, but humbled him in his own eyes, which is perhaps, of all others, the injury least easy to forgive. It was, however, with an appearance of the profoundest submission that he stood awaiting the approach of the man he had tried so much to injure.

"Mr Wentworth, sir," said Elsworthy, "if I was worth your while, I might think as you were offended with me; but seeing I'm one as is so far beneath you"—he went on with a kind of grin, intended to represent a deprecatory smile, but which would have been a snarl had he dared—"I can't think as you'll bear no malice. May I ask, sir, if there's a-going to be any difference made?"

"In what respect, Elsworthy?" said the Curate, shortly.

"Well, sir, I can't tell," said the Clerk of St Roque's. "If a clergyman was to bear malice, it's in his power to make things very unpleasant. I don't speak of the place at church, which ain't neither here nor there—it's respectable, but it ain't lucrative; but if you was to stretch a point, Mr Wentworth, by continuing the papers and suchlike—it ain't that I valley the money," said Elsworthy, "but I've been a faithful servant; and I might say, if you was to take it in a right spirit, an 'umble friend, Mr Wentworth," he continued, after a little pause, growing bolder. "And now, as I've that unfortunate creature to provide for, and no one knowing what's to become of her——"

"I wonder that you venture to speak of her

to me," said the Curate, with a little indignation, "after all the warnings I gave you. But you ought to consider that you are to blame a great deal more than she is. She is only a child; if you had taken better care of her—but you would not pay any attention to my warning;—you must bear the consequences as you best can."

"Well, sir," said Elsworthy, "if you're a-going to bear malice, I haven't got nothing to say. But there ain't ten men in Carlingford as wouldn't agree with me that when a young gentleman, even if he is a clergyman, takes particklar notice of a pretty young girl, it ain't just for nothing as he does it—not to say watching over her paternal to see as she wasn't out late at night, and suchlike. But bygones is bygones, sir," said Elsworthy, "and is never more to be mentioned by me. I don't ask no more, if you'll but do the same——"

"You won't ask no more?" said the Curate, angrily; "do you think I am afraid of you? I have nothing more to say, Elsworthy. Go and look after your business—I will attend to mine; and when we are not forced to meet, let us keep clear of each other. It will be better both for you and me."

The Curate passed on with an impatient nod; but his assailant did not intend that he should escape so easily. "I shouldn't have thought, sir, as you'd have borne malice," said Elsworthy, hastening on after him, yet keeping half a step behind. "I'm a humbled man—different from what I ever thought to be. I could always keep up my head afore the world till now; and if it ain't your fault, sir—as I humbly beg your pardon for ever being so far led away as to believe it was—all the same it's along of you."

"What do you mean?" said the Curate, who, half amused and half indignant at the change of tone, had slackened his pace to listen to this new accusation.

"What I mean, sir, is, that if you hadn't been so good and so kind-hearted as to take into your house the—the villain as has done it all, him and Rosa could never have known each other. I allow as it was nothing but your own goodness as did it; but it was a black day for me and mine," said the dramatist, with a pathetic turn of voice. "Not as I'm casting no blame on you, as is well known to be——"

"Never mind what I'm well known to be," said the Curate; "the other day you thought *I* was the villain. If you can tell me anything you want me to do, I will understand that—but I am not desirous to know your opinion of me," said the careless young man. As he stood listening impatiently, pausing a second time, Dr Marjoribanks came out to his door and stepped into his brougham to go off to his morning round of visits. The Doctor took off his hat when he saw the Curate, and waved it to him cheerfully with a gesture of congratulation. Dr Marjoribanks was quite stanch and honest, and would have manfully stood by his intimates in dangerous circumstances; but somehow he preferred success. It was pleasanter to be able to congratulate people than to condole with them. He preferred it, and nobody could object to so orthodox a sentiment. Most probably, if Mr Wentworth had still been in partial disgrace, the Doctor would not have seen him in his easy glance down the road; but though Mr Wentworth was aware of that, the mute congratulation had yet its effect upon him. He was moved by that delicate symptom of how the wind was blowing in Carlingford, and forgot all about Elsworthy, though the man was standing by his side.

"As you're so good as to take it kind, sir," said the Clerk of St Roque's—"and, as I was a-saying, it's well known as you're always ready to hear a poor man's tale—perhaps you'd let bygones be bygones, and not make no difference? That wasn't all, Mr Wentworth," he continued eagerly, as the Curate gave an impatient nod, and turned to go on. "I've heard as this villain is rich, sir, by means of robbing of his own flesh and blood;—but it ain't for me to trust to what folks says, after the experience I've had, and never can forgive myself for being led away," said Elsworthy; "it's well known in Carlingford——"

"For heaven's sake come to the point and be done with it," said the Curate. "What is it you want me to do?"

"Sir," said Elsworthy, solemnly, "you're a real gentleman, and you don't bear no malice for what was a mistake—and you ain't one to turn your back on an unfortunate family—and Mr Wentworth, sir, you ain't a-going to stand by and see me and mine wronged, as have always wished you well. If we can't get justice of him, we can get damages," cried Elsworthy. "He ain't to be let off as if he'd done no harm—and seeing as it was along of you——"

"Hold your tongue, sir!" cried the Curate. "I have nothing to do with it. Keep out of my way, or at least learn to restrain your tongue. No more—not a word more," said the young man, indignantly. He went off with such a sweep and wind of anger and annoyance, that the slower and older complainant had no chance to follow him. Elsworthy accordingly went off to the shop, where his errand-boys were waiting for the newspapers, and where Rosa lay up-stairs, weeping, in a dark room, where her enraged aunt had shut her up. Mrs Elsworthy had shut up the poor little pretty wretch, who might have been penitent under better guidance, but who by this time had lost what sense of shame and wrong her childish conscience was capable of in the stronger present sense of injury and resentment and longing to escape; but the angry aunt, though she could turn the key on poor Rosa's unfortunate little person, could not shut in the piteous sobs which now and then sounded through and through the house, and which converted all the errand-boys without exception into indignant partisans of Rosa, and even moved the heart of Peter Hayles, who could hear them at the back window where he was making up Dr Marjoribanks's prescriptions. As the sense of injury waxed stronger and stronger in Rosa's bosom, she availed herself, like any other irrational, irresponsible creature, of such means of revenging herself and annoying her keepers as occurred to her. "Nobody ever took no care of me," sobbed Rosa. "I never had no father or mother. Oh, I wish I was dead! I wish I was dead!—and nobody wouldn't care!" These utterances, it may be imagined, went to the very heart of the errand-boys, who were collected in a circle, plotting how to release Rosa, when Elsworthy, mortified and furious, came back from his unsuccessful assault on the Curate. They scattered like a covey of little birds before the angry man, who tossed their papers at them, and then strode up the echoing stairs. "If you don't hold your d—d tongue," said Elsworthy, knocking furiously at Rosa's door, "I'll turn you to the door this instant, I will, by ——." Nobody in Carlingford had ever before heard an oath issue from the respectable lips of the Clerk of St Roque's. When he went down into the shop again, the outcries sank into frightened moans. Not much wonder that the entire neighbourhood became as indignant with Elsworthy as it ever had been with the Perpetual Curate. The husband and wife took up their positions in the shop after this, as far apart as was possible from each other, both resenting in silent fury the wrong which the world in general had done them. If Mrs Elsworthy had dared, she would have exhausted her passion in abuse of everybody—of the Curate for not being guilty, of her husband for supposing him to be so, and, to be sure, of Rosa herself, who was the cause of all. But Elsworthy was dangerous, not to be approached or spoken to. He went out about noon to see John Brown, and discuss with him the question of damages; but the occurrences which took place in his absence are not to be mixed up with the present narrative, which concerns Mr Frank Wentworth's visit to Lucy Wodehouse, and has nothing to do with ignoble hates or loves.

The Curate went rapidly on to the green door, which once more looked like a gate of paradise. He did not know in the least what he was going to do or say—he was only conscious of a state of exaltation, a condition of mind which might precede great happiness or great misery, but had nothing in it of the common state of affairs in which people ask each other "How do you do?" Notwithstanding, the fact is, that when Lucy entered that dear familiar drawing-room, where every feature and individual expression of every piece of furniture was as well known to him as if they had been so many human faces, it was only "How do you do?" that the Curate found himself able to say. The two shook hands as demurely as if Lucy had indeed been, according to the deceptive representation of yesterday, as old as aunt Dora; and then she seated herself in her favourite chair, and tried to begin a little conversation about things in general. Even in these three days, nature and youth had done something for Lucy. She had slept and rested, and the unforeseen misfortune which had come in to distract her grief, had roused all the natural strength that was in her. As she was a little nervous about this interview, not knowing what it might end in, Lucy thought it her duty to be as composed and self-commanding as possible, and, in order to avoid all dangerous and exciting subjects, began to talk of Wharfside.

"I have not heard anything for three or four days about the poor woman at No. 10," she said: "I meant to have gone to see her to-day, but somehow one gets so selfish when —when one's mind is full of affairs of one's own."

"Yes," said the Curate; "and, speaking of that, I wanted to tell you how much comfort your letter had been to me. My head, too, has been very full of affairs of my own. I thought at one time that my friends were forsaking me. It was very good of you to write as you did."

Upon which there followed another little pause. "Indeed, the goodness was all on your side," said Lucy, faltering. "If I had ever dreamt how much you were doing for us! but it all came upon me so suddenly. It is impossible ever to express in words one-half of the gratitude we owe you," she said, with restrained enthusiasm. She looked up at him as she spoke with a little glow of natural fervour, which brought the colour to her cheek and the moisture to her eyes. She was not of the disposition to give either thanks or confidence by halves; and even the slight not unpleasant sense of danger which gave piquancy to this interview, made her resolute to express herself fully. She would not suffer herself to stint her gratitude because of the sweet suspicion which would not be quite silenced, that possibly Mr Wentworth looked for something better than gratitude. Not for any consequences, however much they might be to be avoided, could she be shabby enough to refrain from due acknowledgment of devotion so great. Therefore, while the Perpetual Curate was doing all he could to remind himself of his condition, and to persuade himself that it would be utterly wrong and mean of him to speak, Lucy looked up at him, looked him in the face, with her blue eyes shining dewy and sweet through tears of gratitude and a kind of generous admiration; for, like every other woman, she felt herself exalted and filled with a delicious pride in seeing that the man of her unconscious choice had proved himself the best.

The Curate walked to the window, very much as Mr Proctor had done, in the tumult and confusion of his heart, and came back again with what he had to say written clear on his face, without any possibility of mistake. "I must speak," said the young man; "I have no right to speak, I know; if I had attained the height of self-sacrifice and self-denial, I might, I would be silent—but it is impossible now." He came to a break just then, looking at her to see what encouragement he had to go on; but as Lucy did nothing but listen and grow pale, he had to take his own way.

"What I have to say is not anything new," said the Curate, labouring a little in his voice, as was inevitable when affairs had come to such a crisis, "if I were not in the cruelest position possible to a man. I have only an empty love to lay at your feet; I tell it to you only because I am obliged—because, after all, love is worth telling, even if it comes to nothing. I am not going to appeal to your generosity," continued the young man, kneeling down at the table, not by way of kneeling to Lucy, but by way of bringing himself on a level with her, where she sat with her head bent down on her low chair, "or to ask you to bind yourself to a man who has nothing in the world but love to offer you; but after what has been for years, after all the hours I have spent here, I cannot—part—I cannot let you go—without a word——"

And here he stopped short. He had not asked anything, so that Lucy, even had she been able, had nothing to answer; and as for the young lover himself, he seemed to have come to the limit of his eloquence. He kept waiting for a moment, gazing at her in breathless expectation of a response for which his own words had left no room. Then he rose in an indescribable tumult of disappointment and mortification—unable to conclude that all was over, unable to keep silence, yet not knowing what to say.

"I have been obliged to close all the doors of advancement upon myself," said the Curate, with a little bitterness; "I don't know if you understand me. At this moment I have to deny myself the dearest privilege of existence. Don't mistake me, Lucy," he said, after another pause, coming back to her with humility, "I don't venture to say that you would have accepted anything I had to offer; but this I mean, that to have a home for you now—to have a life for you ready to be laid at your feet, whether you would have had it or not;—what right have I to speak of such delights?" cried the young man. "It does not matter to you; and as for me, I have patience—patience to console myself with——"

Poor Lucy, though she was on the verge of tears, which nothing but the most passionate self-restraint could have kept in, could not help a passing sensation of amusement at these words. "Not too much of that either," she said, softly, with a tremulous smile. "But Patience carries the lilies of the saints," said Lucy, with a touch of the sweet asceticism which had once been so charming to the young Anglican. It brought him back like a spell to the common ground on which they used to meet; it brought him back also to his former position on his knee, which was embarrassing to Lucy, though she had not the heart to draw back, nor even to withdraw her hand, which somehow happened to be in Mr Wentworth's way.

"I am but a man," said the young lover. "I would rather have the roses of life—but, Lucy, I am only a Perpetual Curate," he continued, with her hands in his. Her answer was made in the most heartless and indifferent words. She let two big drops—which fell like hail, though they were warmer than any summer rain—drop out of her eyes, and she said, with lips that had some difficulty in enunciating that heartless sentiment, "I don't see that it matters to me——"

Which was true enough, though it did not sound encouraging; and it is dreadful to confess that, for a little while after, neither Skelmersdale, nor Wentworth, nor Mr Proctor's new rectory, nor the no-income of the Perpetual Curacy of St Roque's, had the smallest place in the thoughts of either of these perfectly inconsiderate young people. For half an hour they were an Emperor and Empress seated upon two thrones, to which all the world was subject; and when at the end of that time they began to remember the world, it was but to laugh at it in their infinite youthful superiority. Then it became apparent that to remain in Carlingford, to work at "the district," to carry out all the ancient intentions of well-doing which had been the first bond between them, was, after all, the life of lives;—which was the state of mind they had both arrived at when Miss Wodehouse, who thought they had been too long together under the circumstances, and could not help wondering what Mr Wentworth could be saying, came into the room, rather flurried in her own person. She thought Lucy must have been telling the Curate about Mr Proctor and his hopes, and was, to tell the truth, a little curious how Mr Wentworth would take it, and a little—the very least—ashamed of encountering his critical looks. The condition of mind into which Miss Wodehouse was thrown when she perceived the real state of affairs would be difficult to describe. She was very glad and very sorry, and utterly puzzled how they were to live; and underneath all these varying emotions was a sudden, half-ludicrous, half-humiliating sense of being cast into the shade, which made Mr Proctor's *fiancée* laugh and made her cry, and brought her down altogether off the temporary pedestal upon which she had stepped, not without a little feminine satisfaction. When a woman is going to be married, especially if that marriage falls later than usual, it is natural that she should expect, for that time at least, to be the first and most prominent figure in her little circle. But, alas! what chance could there be for a mild, dove-coloured bride of forty beside a creature of half her age, endued with all the natural bloom and natural interest of youth?

Miss Wodehouse could not quite make out her own feelings on the subject. "Don't you think if you had waited a little it would have been wiser?" she said, in her timid way; and then kissed her young sister, and said, "I am so glad, my darling—I am sure dear papa would have been pleased," with a sob which brought back to Lucy the grief from which she had for the moment escaped. Under all the circumstances, however, it may well be supposed that it was rather hard upon Mr Wentworth to recollect that he had engaged to return to luncheon with the Squire, and to prepare himself, after this momentous morning's work, to face all the complications of the family, where still Skelmersdale and Wentworth were hanging in the balance, and where the minds of his kith and kin were already too full of excitement to leave much room for another event. He went away reluctantly enough out of the momentary paradise where his Perpetual Curacy was a matter of utter indifference, if not a tender pleasantry, which rather increased than diminished the happiness of the moment—into the ordinary daylight world, where it was a very serious matter, and where what the young couple would have to live upon became the real question to be considered. Mr Wentworth met Wodehouse as he went out, which did not mend matters. The vagabond was loitering about in the garden, attended by one of Elsworthy's errand-boys, with whom he was in earnest conversation, and stopped in his talk to give a sulky nod and "Good morning," to which the Curate had no desire to respond more warmly than was necessary. Lucy was thinking of nothing but himself, and perhaps a little of the "great work" at Wharfside, which her father's illness and death had interrupted; but Mr Wentworth, who was only a man, remembered that Tom Wodehouse would be his brother-in-law with a distinct sensation of disgust, even in the moment of his triumph—which is one instance of the perennial inequality between the two halves of mankind. He had to brace himself up to the encounter of all his people, while she had to meet nothing less delightful than her own dreams. This was how matters came to an issue in respect of Frank Wentworth's personal happiness. His worldly affairs were all astray as yet, and he had not the most distant indication of any gleam of light dawning upon the horizon which could reconcile his duty and honour with good fortune and the delights of life. Meanwhile other discussions were going on in Carlingford, of vital importance to the two young people who had made up their minds to cast themselves upon Providence. And among the various conversations which were being carried on about the same moment in respect to Mr Wentworth—whose affairs, as was natural, were extensively canvassed in Grange Lane, as well as in other less exclusive quarters—it would be wrong to omit a remarkable consultation which took place in the Rectory, where Mrs Morgan sat in the midst of the great bouquets of the drawing-room carpet, making up her first matrimonial difficulty. It would be difficult to explain what influence the drawing-room carpet in the Rectory had on the fortunes of the Perpetual Curate; but when Mr Wentworth's friends come to hear the entire outs and ins of the business, it will be seen that it was not for nothing that Mr Proctor covered the floor of that pretty apartment with roses and lilies half a yard long.

CHAPTER XLIII.

These were eventful days in Grange Lane, when gossip was not nearly rapid enough to follow the march of events. When Mr Wentworth went to lunch with his family, the two sisters kept together in the drawing-room, which seemed again re-consecrated to the purposes of life. Lucy had not much inclination just at that moment to move out of her chair; she was not sociable, to tell the truth, nor disposed to talk even about the new prospects which were brightening over both. She even took out her needlework, to the disgust of her sister. "When there are so many things to talk about, and so much to be considered," Miss Wodehouse said, with a little indignation; and wondered within herself whether Lucy was really insensible to "what had happened," or whether the sense of duty was strong upon her little sister even in the height of her happiness. A woman of greater experience or discrimination might have perceived that Lucy had retired into that sacred silence, sweetest of all youthful privileges, in which she could dream over to herself the wonderful hour which had just come to an end, and the fair future of which it was the gateway. As for Miss Wodehouse herself, she was in a flutter, and could not get over the sense of haste and confusion which this last new incident had brought upon her. Things were going too fast around her, and the timid woman was out of breath. Lucy's composure at such a moment, and, above all, the production of her needlework, was beyond the comprehension of the elder sister.

"My dear," said Miss Wodehouse, with an effort, "I don't doubt that these poor people are badly off, and I am sure it is very good of you to work for them; but if you will only think how many things there are to do! My darling, I am afraid you will have to—to make your own dresses in future, which is what I never thought to see," she said, putting her handkerchief to her eyes; "and we have not had any talk about anything, Lucy, and there are so many things to think of!" Miss Wodehouse, who was moving about the room as she spoke, began to lift her own books and special property off the centre table. The books were principally ancient Annuals in pretty bindings, which no representation on Lucy's part could induce her to think out of date; and among her other possessions was a little desk in Indian mosaic, of ivory, which had been an institution in the house from Lucy's earliest recollection. "And these are yours, Lucy dear," said Miss Wodehouse, standing up on a chair to take down from the wall two little pictures which hung side by side. They were copies both, and neither of great value; one representing the San Sisto Madonna, and the other a sweet St Agnes, whom Lucy had in her earlier days taken to her heart. Lucy's slumbering attention was roused by this sacrilegious act. She gave a little scream, and dropped her work out of her hands.

"What do I mean?" said Miss Wodehouse; "indeed, Lucy dear, we must look it in the face. It is not our drawing-room any longer, you know." Here she made a pause, and sighed; but somehow a vision of the other drawing-room which was awaiting her in the new rectory, made the prospect less doleful than it might have been. She cleared up in a surprising way as she turned to look at her own property on the table. "My cousin Jack gave me this," said the gentle woman, brushing a little dust off her pretty desk. "When it came first, there was nothing like it in Carlingford, for that was before Colonel Chiley and those other Indian people had settled here. Jack was rather fond of me in those days, you know, though I never cared for him," the elder sister continued, with a smile. "Poor fellow! they said he was not very happy when he married." Though this was rather a sad fact, Miss Wodehouse announced it not without a certain gentle satisfaction. "And, Lucy dear, it is our duty to put aside our own things; they were all presents, you know," she said, standing up on the chair again to reach down the St Agnes, which, ever since Lucy had been confirmed, had hung opposite to her on the wall.

"Oh, don't, don't!" cried Lucy. In that little bit of time, not more than five minutes as it appeared, the familiar room, which had just heard the romance of her youth, had come to have a dismantled and desolated look. The agent of this destruction, who saw in her mind's eye a new scene, altogether surpassing the old, looked complacently upon her work, and piled the abstracted articles on the top of each other, with a pleasant sense of property.

"And your little chair and work-table are yours," said Miss Wodehouse; "they were always considered yours. You worked the chair yourself, though perhaps Miss Gibbons helped you a little; and the table, you know, was sent home the day you were eighteen. It was—a present, you remember. Don't cry, my darling, don't cry; oh, I am sure I did not mean anything!" cried Miss Wodehouse, putting down the St Agnes and flying to her sister, about whom she threw her arms. "My hands are all dusty, dear," said the repentant woman; "but you know, Lucy, we must look it in the face, for it is not our drawing-room now. Tom may come in any day and say—oh, dear, dear, here is some one coming up-stairs!"

Lucy extricated herself from her sister's arms when she heard footsteps outside. "If it is anybody who has a right to come, I suppose we are able to receive them," she said, and sat erect over her needlework, with a changed countenance, not condescending so much as to look towards the door.

"But what if it should be Tom? Oh, Lucy

dear, don't be uncivil to him," said the elder sister. Miss Wodehouse even made a furtive attempt to replace the things, in which she was indignantly stopped by Lucy. "But, my dear, perhaps it is Tom," said the alarmed woman, and sank trembling into a chair against the St Agnes, which had just been deposited there.

"It does not matter who it is," said Lucy, with dignity. For her own part, she felt too much aggrieved to mention his name—aggrieved by her own ignorance, by the deception that had been practised upon her, by the character of the man whom she was obliged to call her brother, and chiefly by his existence, which was the principal grievance of all. Lucy's brief life had been embellished, almost ever since she had been capable of independent action, by deeds and thoughts of mercy. With her whole heart she was a disciple of Him who came to seek the lost; notwithstanding, a natural human sentiment in her heart protested against the existence of this man, who had brought shame and distress into the family without any act of theirs, and who injured everybody he came in contact with. When the thought of Rosa Elsworthy occurred to her, a burning blush came upon Lucy's cheek—why were such men permitted in God's world? To be sure, when she came to be aware of what she was thinking, Lucy felt guilty, and called herself a Pharisee, and said a prayer in her heart for the man who had upset all her cherished ideas of her family and home; but, after all, *that* was an afterthought, and did not alter her instinctive sense of repulsion and indignation. All this swept rapidly through her mind while she sat awaiting the entrance of the person or persons who were approaching the door. "If it is the—the owner of the house, it will be best to tell him what things you mean to remove," said Lucy; and before Miss Wodehouse could answer, the door was opened. They started, however, to perceive not Wodehouse, but a personage of very different appearance, who came in with an easy air of polite apology, and looked at them with eyes which recalled to Lucy the eyes which had been gazing into her own scarcely an hour ago. "Pardon me," said this unlooked-for visitor; "your brother, Miss Wodehouse, finds some difficulty in explaining himself to relations from whom he has been separated so long. Not to interfere with family privacy, will you let me assist at the conference?" said Jack Wentworth. "My brother, I understand, is a friend of yours, and your brother—is a—hem—a friend of mine," the diplomatist added, scarcely able to avoid making a wry face over the statement. Wodehouse came in behind, looking an inch or two taller for that acknowledgment, and sat down, confronting his sisters, who were standing on the defensive. The heir, too, had a strong sense of property, as was natural, and the disarrangement of the room struck him in that point of view, especially as Miss Wodehouse continued to prop herself up against the St Agnes in the back of her chair. Wodehouse looked from the wall to the table, and saw what appeared to him a clear case of intended spoliation. "By Jove! they didn't mean to go empty-handed," said the vagabond, who naturally judged according to his own standard, and knew no better. Upon which Lucy, rising with youthful state and dignity, took the explanation upon herself.

"I do not see why we should have the mortification of a spectator," said Lucy, who already, having been engaged three-quarters of an hour, felt deeply disinclined to reveal the weak points of her own family to the inspection of the Wentworths. "All that there is to explain can be done very simply. Thank you,

I will not sit down. Up to this time we may be allowed to imagine ourselves in our own—in our father's house. What we have to say is simple enough."

"But pardon me, my dear Miss Wodehouse——" said Jack Wentworth.

"My sister is Miss Wodehouse," said Lucy. "What there is to settle had better be arranged with our—our brother. If he will tell us precisely when he wishes us to go away, we shall be ready. Mary is going to be married," she went on, turning round so as to face Wodehouse, and addressing him pointedly, though she did not look at him—to the exclusion of Jack, who, experienced man as he was, felt disconcerted, and addressed himself with more precaution to a task which was less easy than he supposed.

"Oh, Lucy!" cried Miss Wodehouse, with a blush worthy of eighteen. It was perhaps the first time that the fact had been so broadly stated, and the sudden announcement made before two men overwhelmed the timid woman. Then she was older than Lucy, and had picked up in the course of her career one or two inevitable scraps of experience, and she could not but wonder with a momentary qualm what Mr Proctor might think of his brother-in-law. Lucy, who thought Mr Proctor only too well off, went on without regarding her sister's exclamation.

"I do not know when the marriage is to be —I don't suppose they have fixed it yet," said Lucy; "but it appears to me that it would save us all some trouble if we were allowed to remain until that time. I do not mean to ask any favour," she said, with a little more sharpness and less dignity. "We could pay rent for that matter, if—if it were desired. She is your sister," said Lucy, suddenly looking Wodehouse in the face, "as well as mine. I daresay she has done as much for you as she has for me. I don't ask any favour for her—but I would cut off my little finger if that would please her," cried the excited young woman, with a wildness of illustration so totally out of keeping with the matter referred to, that Miss Wodehouse, in the midst of her emotion, could scarcely restrain a scream of terror; "and you too might be willing to do something; you cannot have any kind of feeling for me," Lucy continued, recovering herself; "but you might perhaps have some feeling for Mary. If we can be permitted to remain until her marriage takes place, it may perhaps bring about—a feeling—more like—relations; and I shall be able to——"

"Forgive you," Lucy was about to say, but fortunately stopped herself in time; for it was the fact of his existence that she had to forgive, and naturally such an amount of toleration was difficult to explain. As for Wodehouse himself, he listened to this appeal with very mingled feelings. Some natural admiration and liking woke in his dull mind as Lucy spoke. He was not destitute of good impulses, nor of the ordinary human affections. His little sister was pretty, and a lady, and clever enough to put Jack Wentworth much more in the background than usual. He said "By Jove" to himself three or four times over in his beard, and showed a little emotion when she said he could have no feeling for her. At that point of Lucy's address he moved about uneasily in his chair, and plucked at his beard, and felt himself anything but comfortable. "By Jove! I never had a chance," the prodigal said, in his undertone. "I might have cared a deal for her if I had had a chance. She might have done a fellow good, by Jove!" mutterings of which Lucy took no manner of notice, but proceeded with her speech. When she had ended, and it became apparent that an answer was expected of him, Wodehouse flushed all over with the embarrassment of the position. He cleared his throat, he shifted his eyes, which were embarrassed by Lucy's gaze, he pushed his chair from the table, and made various attempts to collect himself, but at last ended by a pitiful appeal to Jack Wentworth, who had been looking seriously on. "You might come to a fellow's assistance!" cried Wodehouse. "By Jove! it was for that you came here."

"The Miss Wodehouses evidently prefer to communicate with their brother direct," said Jack Wentworth, "which is a very natural sentiment. If I interfere, it is simply because I have had the advantage of talking the matter over, and understanding a little what you mean. Miss Wodehouse, your brother is not disposed to act the part of a domestic tyrant. He has come here to offer you the house, which must have so many tender associations for you, not for a short period, as you wish, but for——"

"I didn't know she was going to be married!" exclaimed Wodehouse—"that makes all the difference, by Jove! Lucy will marry fast enough; but as for Mary, I never thought she would hook any one at her time of life," said the vagabond, with a rude laugh. He turned to Lucy, not knowing any better, and with some intention of pleasing her; but being met by a look of indignation under which he faltered, he went back to his natural rôle of sulky insolence. "By Jove! when I gave in to make such an offer, I never thought she had a chance of getting married," said the heir. "I ain't going to give what belongs to me to another man——"

"Your brother wishes," said Jack Wentworth, calmly, "to make over the house and furniture as it stands to you and your sister, Miss Wodehouse. Of course it is not to be expected that he should be sorry to get his father's property; but he is sorry that there should be no—no provision for you. He means that you should have the house——"

"But I never thought she was going to be married, by Jove!" protested the rightful owner. "Look here, Molly; you shall have the furniture. The house would sell for a good bit of money. I tell you, Wentworth——"

Jack Wentworth did not move from the mantelpiece where he was standing, but he cast a glance upon his unlucky follower which froze the words on his lips. "My good fellow, you are quite at liberty to decline my mediation in your affairs. Probably you can manage them better your own way," said Wodehouse's hero.

"I can only beg the Miss Wodehouses to pardon my intrusion." Jack Wentworth's first step towards the door let loose a flood of nameless terrors upon the soul of his victim. If he were abandoned by his powerful protector, what would become of him? His very desire of money, and the avarice which prompted him to grudge making any provision for his sisters, was, after all, not real avarice, but the spendthrift's longing for more to spend. The house which he was sentenced to give up represented not so much gold and silver, but so many pleasures, fine dinners, and bad company. He could order the dinners by himself, it is true, and get men like himself to eat them; but the fine people—the men who had once been fine, and who still retained a certain tarnished glory—were, so far as Wodehouse was concerned, entirely in Jack Wentworth's keeping. He made a piteous appeal to his patron as the great man turned to go away.

"I don't see what good it can do *you* to rob a poor fellow!" cried Wodehouse. "But look here, I ain't going to turn against your advice. I'll give it them, by Jove, for life—that is, for Mary's life," said the munificent brother. "She's twenty years older than Lucy——"

"How do you dare to subject us to such insults?" cried the indignant Lucy, whose little hand clenched involuntarily in her passion. She had a great deal of self-control, but she was not quite equal to such an emergency; and it was all she could do to keep from stamping her foot, which was the only utterance of rage possible to a gentlewoman in her position. "I would rather see my father's house desecrated by you living in it," she cried, passionately, "than accept it as a gift from your hands. Mary, we are not obliged to submit to this. Let us rather go away at once. I will not remain in the same room with this man!" cried Lucy. She was so overwhelmed with her unwonted passion that she lost all command of the position, and even of herself, and was false for the moment to all her sweet codes of womanly behaviour. "How dare you, sir!" she cried, in the sudden storm, for which nobody was prepared. "We will remove the things belonging to us, with which nobody has any right to interfere, and we will leave immediately. Mary, come with me!" When she had said this, Lucy swept out of the room, pale as a little fury, and feeling in her heart a savage female inclination to strike Jack Wentworth, who opened the door for her, with her little white clenched hand. Too much excited to remark whether her sister had followed her, Lucy ran up-stairs to her room, and there gave way to the inevitable tears. Coming to herself after that was a terribly humbling process to the little Anglican. She had never fallen into a "passion" before that she knew of, certainly never since nursery times; and often enough her severe serene girlhood had looked reproving and surprised upon the tumults of Prickett's Lane, awing the belligerents into at least temporary silence. Now poor Lucy sat and cried over her downfall; she had forgotten herself; she had been conscious of an inclination to stamp, to scold, even to strike, in the vehemence of her indignation; and she was utterly overpowered by the thought of her guiltiness. "The very first temptation!" she said to herself; and made terrible reflections upon her own want of strength and endurance. To-day, too, of all days, when God had been so good to her! "If I yield to the first temptation like this, how shall I ever endure to the end?" cried Lucy, and in her heart thought, with a certain longing, of the sacrament of penance, and tried to think what she could do that would be most disagreeable, to the mortifying of the flesh. Perhaps if she had possessed a more lively sense of humour, another view of the subject might have struck Lucy; but humour, fortunately for the unity of human sentiment, is generally developed at a later period of life, and Lucy's fit of passion only made her think with greater tenderness and toleration of her termagants in Prickett's Lane.

The three who were left down-stairs were in their different ways impressed by Lucy's passion. Jack Wentworth, being a man of humour and cultivation, was amused, but respectful, as having still a certain faculty of appreciating absolute purity when he saw it. As for Wodehouse, he gave another rude laugh, but was cowed in spite of himself, and felt involuntarily what a shabby wretch he was, recognising that fact more impressively from the contempt of Lucy's pale face than he could have done through hours of argument. Miss Wodehouse, for her part, though very anxious and nervous, was not without an interest in the question under discussion. *She* was not specially horrified by her brother, or anything he could say or do. He was Tom to her—a boy with whom she had once played, and whom she had shielded with all her sisterly might in his first transgressions. She had suffered a great deal more by his means than Lucy could ever suffer, and consequently was more tolerant of him. She kept her seat with the St Agnes in the chair behind, and watched the course of events with anxious steadiness. She did not care for money any more than Lucy did; but she could not help thinking it would be very pleasant if she could produce one good action on "poor Tom's" part to plead for him against any possible criticisms of the future. Miss Wodehouse was old enough to know that her Rector was not an ideal hero, but an ordinary man, and it was quite possible that he might point a future moral now and then with "that brother of yours, my dear." The elder sister waited accordingly, with her heart beating quick, to know the decision, very anxious that she might have at least one generous deed to record to the advantage of poor Tom.

"I think we are quite decided on the point," said Jack Wentworth. "Knowing your sentiments, Wodehouse, I left directions with Waters about the papers. I think you will find him quite to be trusted, Miss Wodehouse, if you wish to consult him about letting or selling——"

"By Jove!" exclaimed Wodehouse, under his breath.

"Which, I suppose," continued the superb Jack, "you will wish to do under the pleasant circumstances, upon which I beg to offer you my congratulations. Now, Tom, my good fellow, I am at your service. I think we have done our business here."

Wodehouse got up in his sulking reluctant way like a lazy dog. "I suppose you won't try to move the furniture now?" he said. These were the only adieux he intended to make, and perhaps they might have been expressed with still less civility, had not Jack Wentworth been standing waiting for him at the door.

"Oh, Tom! I am so thankful you have done it," cried Miss Wodehouse. "It is not that I care for the money; but oh, Tom, I am so glad to think nobody can say anything now." She followed them wistfully to the door, not giving up hopes of a kinder parting. "I think it is very kind and nice of you, and what dear papa would have wished," said the elder sister, forgetting how all her father's plans had been brought to nothing; "and of course you will live here all the same?" she said, with a little eagerness, "that is, till—till—as long as we are here——"

"Good-bye, Miss Wodehouse," said Jack Wentworth. "I don't think either your brother or I will stay much longer in Carlingford. You must accept my best wishes for your happiness all the same."

"You are very kind, I am sure," said the embarrassed bride; "and oh, Tom, you will surely say good-bye? Say good-bye once as if you meant it; don't go away as if you did not care. Tom, I always was very fond of you; and don't you feel a little different to us, now you've done us a kindness?" cried Miss Wodehouse, going out after him to the landing-place. But Wodehouse was in no humour to be gracious. Instead of paying any attention to her, he looked regretfully at the property he had lost.

"Good-bye," he said, vaguely. "By Jove! I know better than Jack Wentworth does the value of property. We might have had a jolly month at Homburg out of that old place," said the prodigal, with regret, as he went down the old-fashioned oak stair. That was his farewell to the house which he had entered so disastrously on the day of his father's funeral. He followed his leader with a sulky aspect through the garden, not venturing to disobey, but yet feeling the weight of his chains. And this was how Wodehouse accomplished his personal share in the gift to his sisters, of which Miss Wodehouse told everybody that it was "so good of Tom!"

CHAPTER XLIV.

"Going to be married!" said the Squire; "and to a sister of—— I thought you told me she was as old as Dora, Frank? I did not expect to meet with any further complications," the old man said, plaintively; "of course you know very well I don't object to your marrying; but why on earth did you let me speak of Wentworth Rectory to Huxtable?" cried Mr Wentworth. He was almost more impatient about this new variety in the family circumstances than he had been of more serious distresses. "God bless me, sir," said the Squire, "what do you mean by it? You take means to affront your aunts and lose Skelmersdale; and then you put it into my head to have Mary at Wentworth; and then you quarrel with the Rector, and get into hot water in Carlingford; and, to make an end of all, you coolly propose to an innocent young woman, and tell me you are going to marry — what on earth do you mean?"

"I am going to marry some time, sir, I hope," said the Perpetual Curate, with more cheerfulness than he felt; "but not at the present moment. Of course we both know that is impossible. I should like you to come with me and see her before you leave Carlingford. She would like it, and so should I."

"Well, well," said the Squire. Naturally, having been married so often himself, he could not refuse a certain response to such a call upon his sympathy. "I hope you have made a wise choice," said the experienced father, not without a sigh; "a great deal depends upon that—not only your own comfort, sir, but very often the character of your children and the credit of the family. You may laugh," said Mr Wentworth, to whom it was no laughing matter; "but long before you are as old as I am, you will know the truth of what I say. Your mother, Frank, was a specimen of what a woman ought to be—not to speak of her own children, there was nobody else who ever knew how to manage Gerald and Jack. Of course I am not speaking of Mrs Wentworth, who has her nursery to occupy her," said the Squire, apologetically. "I hope you have made a judicious choice."

"I hope so too," said Frank, who was somewhat amused by this view of the question—"though I am not aware of having exercised any special choice in the matter," he added, with a laugh. "However, I want you to come with me and see her, and then you will be able to judge for yourself."

The Squire shook his head, and looked as if he had travelled back into the heavy roll of family distresses. "I don't mean to upbraid you, Frank," he said—"I daresay you have done what you thought was your duty—but I think you might have taken a little pains to satisfy your aunt Leonora. You see what Gerald has made of it, with all his decorations and nonsense. That is a dreadful drawback with you clergymen. You fix your eyes so on one point that you get to think things important that are not in the least important. Could you imagine a man of the world like Jack—he is not what I could wish, but still he is a man of the world," said the Squire, who was capable of contradicting himself with perfect composure without knowing it. "Can you imagine *him* risking his prospects for a bit of external decoration? I don't mind it myself," said Mr Wentworth, impartially—"I don't pretend to see, for my own part, why flowers at Easter should be considered more superstitious than holly at Christmas; but, bless my soul, sir, when your aunt thought so, what was the good of running right in her face for such a trifle? I never could understand you parsons," the Squire said, with an impatient sigh—"nobody, that I know of, ever considered me mercenary; but to ruin your own prospects, all for a trumpery bunch of flowers, and then to come and tell me you want to marry——"

This was before luncheon, when Frank and his father were together in the dining-room waiting for the other members of the family, who began to arrive at this moment, and prevented any further discussion. After all, perhaps, it was a little ungenerous of the Squire to press his son so hard on the subject of those innocent Easter lilies, long ago withered, which certainly, looked at from this distance, did not appear important enough to sacrifice any prospects for. This was all the harder upon the unfortunate Curate, as even at the time his conviction of their necessity had not proved equal to the satisfactory settlement of the question. Miss Wentworth's cook was an *artiste* so irreproachable that the luncheon provided was in itself perfect; but notwithstanding it was an uncomfortable meal. Miss Leonora, in consequence of the contest going on in her own mind, was in an explosive and highly dangerous condition, not safe to be spoken to; and as for the Squire, he could not restrain the chance utterances of his impatience. Frank, who did his best to make himself agreeable as magnanimity required, had the mortification of hearing himself discussed in different tones of disapprobation while he ate his cold beef; for Mr Wentworth's broken sentences were not long of putting the party in possession of the new event, and the Perpetual Curate found himself the object of many wondering and pitying glances, in none of which could he read pure sympathy, much less congratulation. Even Gerald looked at him with a little elevation of his eyebrows, as if wondering how anybody could take the trouble to occupy his mind with such trifling temporal affairs as love and marriage. It was a wonderful relief to the unfortunate Curate when Miss Leonora had finished her glass of madeira, and rose from the table. He had no inclination to go up-stairs, for his own part. "When you are ready, sir, you will find me in the garden," he said to his father, who was to leave Carlingford next morning, and whom he had set his heart on taking to see Lucy. But his walk in the garden was far from being delightful to Frank. It even occurred to him, for a moment, that it would be a very good thing if a man could cut himself adrift from his relations at such a crisis of his life. After all, it was his own business—the act most essentially personal of his entire existence; and then, with a little softening, he began to think of the girls at home —of the little sister, who had a love-story of her own; and of Letty, who was Frank's favourite, and had often confided to him the enthusiasm she would feel for his bride. "If she is nice," Letty was in the habit of adding, "and of course she will be nice,"—and at that thought the heart of the young lover escaped, and put forth its wings, and went off into that heaven of ideal excellence and beauty, more sweet, because more vague, than anything real, which stands instead of the old working-day skies and clouds at such a period of life. He had to drop down from a great height, and get rid in all haste of his celestial pinions, when he heard his aunt Dora calling him; and his self-command was not sufficient to conceal, as he obeyed that summons, a certain annoyed expression in his face.

"Frank," said Miss Dora, coming softly after him with her handkerchief held over her head as a defence from the sun—"oh, Frank, I want to speak to you. I couldn't say anything at lunch because of everybody being there. If you would only stop a moment till I get my breath. Frank, my dear boy, I wish you joy. I do wish you joy with all my heart. I should so like just to go and kiss her, and tell her I shall love her for your sake."

"You will soon love her for her own sake," said Frank, to whom even this simple-minded sympathy was very grateful; "she is a great deal better than I am."

"There is just one thing," said Miss Dora. "Oh, Frank, my dear, you know I don't pretend to be clever, like Leonora, or able to give you advice; but there *is* one thing. You know you have nothing to marry upon, and all has gone wrong. You are not to have Wentworth, and you are not to have Skelmersdale, and I think the family is going out of its senses not to see who is the most worthy. You have got nothing to live upon, my dear, dear boy!" said Miss

Dora, withdrawing the handkerchief from her head in the excitement of the moment to apply it to her eyes.

"That is true enough," said the Perpetual Curate; "but then we have not made up our minds that we must marry immediately——"

"Frank," said aunt Dora, with solemnity, breaking into his speech, "there is just *one* thing; and I can't hold my tongue, though it may be very foolish, and they will all say it is my fault." It was a very quiet summer-day, but still there was a faint rustle in the branches which alarmed the timid woman. She put her hand upon her nephew's arm, and hastened him on to the little summer-house in the wall, which was her special retirement. "Nobody ever comes here," said Miss Dora; "they will never think of looking for us here. I am sure I never interfere with Leonora's arrangements, nor take anything upon myself; but there is one thing, Frank——"

"Yes," said the Curate, "I understand what you mean: you are going to warn me about love in a cottage, and how foolish it would be to marry upon nothing; but, my dear aunt, we are not going to do anything rash; there is no such dreadful haste; don't be agitated about it," said the young man, with a smile. He was half amused and half irritated by the earnestness which almost took away the poor lady's breath.

"You *don't* know what I mean," said aunt Dora. "Frank, you know very well I never interfere; but I can't help being agitated when I see you on the brink of such a precipice. Oh, my dear boy, don't be over-persuaded. There *is* one thing, and I must say it if I should die." She had to pause a little to recover her voice, for haste and excitement had a tendency to make her inarticulate. "Frank," said Miss Dora again, more solemnly than ever, "whatever you may be obliged to do—though you were to write novels, or take pupils, or do translations—oh, Frank, don't look at me like that, as if I was going crazy. Whatever you may have to do, oh, my dear, there is one thing—don't go and break people's hearts, and put it off, and put it off, till it never happens!" cried the trembling little woman, with a sudden burst of tears. "Don't say you can wait, for you can't wait, and you oughtn't to!" sobbed Miss Dora. She subsided altogether into her handkerchief and her chair as she uttered this startling and wholly unexpected piece of advice, and lay there in a little heap, all dissolving and floating away, overcome with her great effort, while her nephew stood looking at her from a height of astonishment almost too extreme for wondering. If the trees could have found a voice and counselled his immediate marriage, he could scarcely have been more surprised.

"You think I am losing my senses too," said aunt Dora; "but that is because you don't understand me. Oh Frank, my dear boy, there was once a time!—perhaps everybody has forgotten it except me, but I have not forgotten it. They treated me like a baby, and Leonora had everything her own way. I don't mean to say it was not for the best," said the aggrieved woman. "I know everything is for the best, if we could but see it; and perhaps Leonora was right when she said I never could have struggled with—with a family, nor lived on a poor man's income. My dear, it was before your uncle Charley died; and when we became rich, it—didn't matter," said Miss Dora; "it was all over before then. Oh Frank! if I hadn't experience I wouldn't say a word. I don't interfere about your opinions, like Leonora. There is just *one* thing," cried the poor lady through her tears. Perhaps it was the recollection of the past which overcame Miss Dora, perhaps the force of habit which had made it natural for her to cry when she was much moved; but the fact is certain, that the Squire, when he came to the door of the summer-house in search of Frank, found his sister weeping bitterly, and his son making efforts to console her, in which some sympathy was mingled with a certain half-amusement. Frank, like Lucy, felt tempted to laugh at the elderly romance; and yet his heart expanded warmly to his tender little foolish aunt, who, after all, might once have been young and in love like himself, though it was so odd to realise it. Mr Wentworth, for his part, saw no humour whatever in the scene. He thought nothing less than that some fresh complication had taken place. Jack had committed some new enormity, or there was bad news from Charley in Malta, or unpleasant letters had come from home. "Bless my soul, sir, something new has happened," said the Squire; and he was scarcely reassured, when Miss Dora stumbled up from her chair in great confusion, and wiped the tears from her eyes. He was suspicious of this meeting in the summer-house, which seemed a quite unnecessary proceeding to Mr Wentworth; and though he flattered himself he understood women, he could not give any reasonable explanation to himself of Dora's tears.

"It is nothing—nothing at all," said Miss Dora: "it was not Frank's doing in the least; he is always so considerate, and such a dear fellow. Thank you, my dear boy; my head is a little better; I think I will go in and lie down," said the unlucky aunt. "You are not to mind me now, for I have quite got over my little attack; I always was so nervous," said Miss Dora; "and I sometimes wonder whether it isn't the Wentworth complaint coming on," she added, with a natural female artifice which was not without its effect.

"I wish you would not talk nonsense," said the Squire. "The Wentworth complaint is nothing to laugh at, but you are perfectly aware that it never attacks women." Mr Wentworth spoke with a little natural irritation, displeased to have his prerogative interfered with. When a man has all the suffering attendant upon a special complaint, it is hard not to have all the dignity. He felt so much and so justly annoyed by Miss Dora's vain pretensions, that he forgot his anxiety about the secret conference in the summer-house.

"Women take such fantastic ideas into their heads," he said to his son as they went away together. "Your aunt Dora is the kindest soul in the world; but now and then, sir, she is very absurd," said the Squire. He could not get this presumptuous notion out of his head, but returned to it again and again, even after they had got into Grange Lane. "It has been in our family for two hundred years," said Mr Wentworth; "and I don't think there is a single instance of its attacking a woman—not even slightly, sir," the Squire added, with irritation, as if Frank had taken the part of the female members of the family, which indeed the Curate had no thought of doing.

Miss Dora, for her part, having made this very successful diversion, escaped to the house, and to her own room, where she indulged in a headache all the afternoon, and certain tender recollections which were a wonderful resource at all times to the soft-hearted woman. "Oh, my dear boy, don't be over-persuaded," she had whispered into Frank's ear as she left him; and her remonstrance, simple as it was, had no doubt produced a considerable effect upon the mind of the Perpetual Curate. He could not help thinking, as they emerged into the road, that it was chiefly the impatient and undutiful who secured their own happiness, or what they imagined to be their happiness. Those who were constant and patient, and able to deny themselves, instead of being rewarded for their higher qualities, were, on the contrary, put to the full test of the strength that was in them; while those who would not wait attained what they wanted, and on the whole, as to other matters, got on just as well as their stronger-minded neighbours. This germ of thought, it may be supposed, was stimulated into very warm life by the reflection that Lucy would have to leave Carlingford with her sister, without any definite prospect of returning again; and a certain flush of impatience came over the young man, not unnatural in the circumstances. It seemed to him that everybody else took their own way without waiting; and why should it be so certain that he alone, whose "way" implied harm to no one, should be the only man condemned to wait? Thus it will be seen that the "just one thing" insisted on by Miss Dora was far from being without effect on the mind of her nephew; upon whom, indeed, the events of the morning had wrought various changes of sentiment. When he walked up Grange Lane for the first time, it had been without any acknowledged intention of opening his mind to Lucy, and yet he had returned along the same prosaic and unsympathetic line of road her accepted lover; her accepted lover, triumphant in that fact, but without the least opening of any hope before him as to the conclusion of the engagement, which prudence had no hand in making. Now the footsteps of the Perpetual Curate fell firmly, not to say a little impatiently, upon the road over which he had carried so many varying thoughts. He was as penniless as ever, and as prospectless; but in the tossings of his natural impatience the young man had felt the reins hang loosely about his head, and knew that he was no more restrained than other men, but might, if he chose it, have his way like the rest of the world. It was true enough that he might have to pay for it after, as other people had done; but in the mean time the sense that he was his own master was sweet, and to have his will for once seemed no more than his right in the world. While these rebellious thoughts were going on in the Curate's mind, his father, who suspected nothing, went steadily by his side, not without a little reluctance at thought of the errand on which he was bound. "But they can't marry for years, and nobody can tell what may happen in that time," Mr Wentworth said to himself, with the callousness of mature age, not suspecting the different ideas that were afloat in the mind of his son. Perhaps, on the whole, he was not sorry that Skelmersdale was destined otherwise, and that Huxtable had been spoken to about Wentworth Rectory; for, of course, Frank would have plunged into marriage at once if he had been possessed of anything to marry on; and it looked providential under the circumstances, as the Squire argued with himself privately, that at such a crisis the Perpetual Curate should have fallen between the two stools of possible preferment, and should be still obliged to content himself with St Roque's. It was hard for Mr Wentworth to reconcile himself to the idea that the wife of his favourite son should be the sister of——; for the Squire forgot that his own girls were Jack Wentworth's sisters, and as such might be objected to in their turn by some other father. So the two gentlemen went to see Lucy, who was then in a very humble frame of mind, just recovered from her passion—one of them rather congratulating himself on the obstacles which lay before the young couple, the other tossing his youthful head a little in the first impulses of self-will, feeling the reins lie loose upon him, and making up his mind to have his own way.

CHAPTER XLV.

While Mr Frank Wentworth's affairs were thus gathering to a crisis, other events likely to influence his fate were also taking place in Carlingford. Breakfast had been served a full half-hour later than usual in the Rectory, which had not improved the temper of the household. Everything was going on with the most wonderful quietness in that well-arranged house; but it was a quietness which would have made a sensitive visitor uncomfortable, and which woke horrible private qualms in the mind of the Rector. As for Mrs Morgan, she fulfilled all her duties with a precision which was terrible to behold: instead of taking part in the conversation as usual, and having her own opinion, she had suddenly become possessed of such a spirit of meekness and acquiescence as filled her husband with dismay. The Rector was fond of his wife, and proud of her good sense, and her judgment, and powers of conversation. If she had been angry and found fault with him, he might have understood that mode of procedure; but as she was not angry, but only silent, the excellent man was terribly disconcerted, and could not tell what to do. He had done all he could to be conciliatory, and had already entered upon a great many explanations which had come to nothing for want of any response; and now she sat at the head of the table making tea with an imperturbable countenance, sometimes making little observations about the news, perfectly calm and dignified, but taking no part in anything more interesting, and turning off any reference that was made to her in the most skilful manner. "Mr Morgan knows I never take any part in the gossip of Carlingford," she said to Mr Proctor, without any intention of wounding that good man; and he who had been in the midst of something about Mr Wentworth came to an abrupt stop with the sense of having shown himself a gossip, which was very injurious to his dignity. The late Rector, indeed, occupied a very uncomfortable position between the married people thus engaged in the absorbing excitement of their first quarrel. The quiet little arrows, which Mrs Morgan intended only for her husband, grazed and stung him as they passed, without missing at the same time their intended aim; and he was the auditor, besides, of a great deal of information intended by the Rector for his wife's benefit, to which Mrs Morgan paid no manner of attention. Mr Proctor was not a man of very lively observation, but he could not quite shut his eyes to the position of affairs; and the natural effect upon his mind, in the circumstances, was to turn his thoughts towards his mild Mary, whom he did not quite recognise as yet under her Christian name. He called her Miss Wodehouse in his heart even while in the act of making comparisons very unfavourable to the Rector's wife, and then he introduced benevolently the subject of his new Rectory, which surely must be safe ground.

"It is a pretty little place," Mr Proctor said, with satisfaction: "of course it is but a small living compared to Carlingford. I hope you will come and see me, after—it is furnished," said the bashful bridegroom: "it is a nuisance to have all that to look after for one's self——"

"I hope you will have somebody to help

you," said Mrs Morgan, with a little earnestness; "gentlemen don't understand about such things. When you have one piece of furniture in bad taste, it spoils a whole room—carpets, for instance——" said the Rector's wife. She looked at Mr Proctor so severely that the good man faltered, though he was not aware of the full extent of his guiltiness.

"I am sure I don't know," he said: "I told the man here to provide everything as it ought to be; and I think we were very successful," continued Mr Proctor, with a little complacency: to be sure, they were in the dining-room at the moment, being still at the breakfast-table. "Buller knows a great deal about that sort of thing, but then he is too ecclesiological for my taste. I like things to look cheerful," said the unsuspicious man. "Buller is the only man that could be reckoned on if any living were to fall vacant. It is very odd nowadays how indifferent men are about the Church. I don't say that it is not very pleasant at All-Souls; but a house of one's own, you know——" said Mr Proctor, looking with a little awkward enthusiasm at his recently married brother; "of course I mean a sphere—a career——"

"Oh, ah, yes," said Mr Morgan, with momentary gruffness; "but everything has its drawbacks. I don't think Buller would take a living. He knows too well what's comfortable," said the suffering man. "The next living that falls will have to go to some one out of the College," said Mr Morgan. He spoke with a tone of importance and significance which moved Mr Proctor, though he was not very rapid in his perceptions, to look across at him for further information.

"Most people have some crotchet or other," said the Rector. "When a man's views are clear about subscription, and that sort of thing, he generally goes as far wrong the other way. Buller might go out to Central Africa, perhaps, if there was a bishopric of Wahuma—or what is the name, my dear, in that Nile book?"

"I have not read it," said Mrs Morgan, and she made no further remark.

Thus discouarged in his little attempt at amity, the Rector resumed after a moment, "Wentworth's brother has sent in his resignation to his bishop. There is no doubt about it any longer. I thought that delusion had been over, at all events; and I suppose now Wentworth will be provided for," said Mr Morgan, not without a little anxiety.

"No; they are all equally crotchety, I think," said Mr Proctor. "I know about them, through my—my connection with the Wodehouses, you know. I should not wonder, for my own part, if he went after his brother, who is a very intelligent man, though mistaken," the late Rector added, with respect. "As for Frank Wentworth, he is a little hot-headed. I had a long conversation the other night with the elder brother. I tried to draw him out about Burgon's book, but he declined to enter into the question. Frank has made up his mind to stay in Carlingford. I understand he thinks it right on account of his character being called in question here; though, of course, no one in his senses could have had any doubt how *that* would turn out," said Mr Proctor, forgetting that he himself had been very doubtful about the Curate. "From what I hear, they are all very crotchety," he continued, and finished his breakfast calmly, as if that settled the question. As for Mrs Morgan, even this interesting statement had no effect upon her. She looked up suddenly at one moment as if intending to dart a reproachful glance at her husband, but bethought herself in time, and remained passive as before; not the less, however, was she moved by what she had just heard. It was not Mr Wentworth she was thinking of, except in a very secondary degree. What occupied her, and made her reflections bitter, was the thought that her husband—the man to whom she had been faithful for ten weary years—had taken himself down off the pedestal on which she had placed him. "To make idols, and to find them clay," she said plaintively in her own mind. Women were all fools to spend their time and strength in constructing such pedestals, Mrs Morgan thought to herself with bitterness; and as to the men who were so perpetually dethroning themselves, how were they to be designated? To think of her William, of whom she had once made a hero, ruining thus, for a little petty malice and rivalry, the prospects of another man! While these painful reflections were going through her mind, she was putting away her tea-caddy, and preparing to leave the gentlemen to their own affairs. "We shall see you at dinner at six," she said, with a constrained little smile, to Mr Proctor, and went up-stairs with her key-basket in her hand without taking any special notice of the Rector.

Mr Leeson was to come to dinner that day legitimately by invitation, and Mrs Morgan, who felt it would be a little consolation to disappoint the hungry Curate for once, was making up her mind, as she went up-stairs, not to have the All-Souls pudding, of which he showed so high an appreciation. It almost seemed to her as if this spark of ill-nature was receiving a summary chastisement, when she heard steps ascending behind her. Mrs Morgan objected to have men lounging about her drawing-room in the morning. She thought Mr Proctor was coming to bestow a little more of his confidence upon her, and perhaps to consult her about his furnishing; and being occupied by her own troubles, she had no patience for a tiresome, middle-aged lover, who no doubt was going to disappoint and disenchant another woman. She sat down, accordingly, with a sigh of impatience at her work-table, turning her back to the door. Perhaps, when he saw her inhospitable attitude, he might go away and not bother her. And Mrs Morgan took out some stockings to darn, as being a discontented occupation, and was considering within herself what simple preparation she could have instead of the All-Souls pudding, when, looking up suddenly, she saw, not Mr

Proctor, but the Rector, standing looking down upon her within a few steps of her chair. When she perceived him, it was not in nature to refrain from certain symptoms of agitation. The thoughts she had been indulging in brought suddenly a rush of guilty colour to her face; but she commanded herself as well as she could, and went on darning her stockings, with her heart beating very loud in her breast.

"My dear," said the Rector, taking a seat near her, "I don't know what it is that has risen up between us. We look as if we had quarrelled; and I thought we had made up our minds never to quarrel." The words were rather soft in their signification, but Mr Morgan could not help speaking severely, as was natural to his voice; which was perhaps, in the present case, all the better for his wife.

"I don't know what you may consider quarrelling, William," said Mrs Morgan, "but I am sure I have never made any complaint."

"No," said the Rector; "I have seen women do that before. You don't make any complaint, but you look as if you disapproved of everything. I feel it all the more just now because I want to consult you; and, after all, the occasion was no such——"

"I never said there was any occasion. I am sure I never made any complaint. You said you wanted to consult me, William?" Mrs Morgan went on darning her stockings while she was speaking, and the Rector, like most other men, objected to be spoken to by the lips only. He would have liked to toss the stocking out of the window, though it was his own, and the task of repairing it was one of a devoted wife's first duties, according to the code of female proprieties in which both the husband and wife had been brought up.

"Yes," said the Rector, with a sigh. "The truth is, I have just got a letter from Harry Scarsfield, who was my pet pupil long ago. He tells me my father's old rectory is vacant, where we were all brought up. There used to be constant intercourse between the Hall and the Rectory when I was a lad. They are very nice people the Scarsfields—at least they used to be very nice people; and Harry has his mother living with him, and the family has never been broken up, I believe. We used to know everybody about there," said Mr Morgan, abandoning himself to recollections in a manner most mysterious to his wife. "There is the letter, my dear," and he put it down upon her table, and began to play with the reels of cotton in her workbox unconsciously, as he had not done for a long time; which, unawares to herself, had a softening influence upon Mrs Morgan's heart.

"I do not know anything about the Scarsfields," she said, without taking up the letter, "and I cannot see what you have to do with this. Does he wish you to recommend some one?" Mrs Morgan added, with a momentary interest; for she had, of course, like other people, a relation in a poor living, whom it would have been satisfactory to recommend.

"He says I may have it if I have a mind," said the Rector, curtly, betraying a little aggravation in his tone.

"You, William?" said Mrs Morgan. She was so much surprised that she laid down her stocking and looked him straight in the face, which she had not done for many days; and it was wonderful how hard she found it to keep up her reserve, after having once looked her husband in the eyes. "But it is not much more than six months since you were settled in Carlingford," she said, still lost in amazement. "You cannot possibly mean to make a change so soon? and then the difference of the position," said the Rector's wife. As she looked at him, she became more and more aware of some meaning in his face which she did not understand; and more and more, as it became necessary to understand him, the reserves and self-defences of the first quarrel gave way and dispersed. "I don't think I quite know what you mean," she said, faltering a little. "I don't understand why you should think of a change."

"A good country living is a very good position," said the Rector; "it is not nearly so troublesome as a town like Carlingford. There is no Dissent that I know of, and no——" (here Mr Morgan paused for a moment, not knowing what word to use)—"no disturbing influences: of course I would not take such a step without your concurrence, my dear," the Rector continued; and then there followed a bewildering pause. Mrs Morgan's first sensation after the astonishment with which she heard this strange proposal was mortification—the vivid shame and vexation of a woman when she is obliged to own to herself that her husband has been worsted, and is retiring from the field.

"If you think it right—if you think it best—of course I can have nothing to say," said the Rector's wife; and she took up her stocking with a stinging sense of discomfiture. She had meant that her husband should be the first man in Carlingford—that he should gain everybody's respect and veneration, and become the ideal parish-priest of that favoured and fortunate place. Every kind of good work and benevolent undertaking was to be connected with his name, according to the visions which Mrs Morgan had framed when she came first to Carlingford, not without such a participation on her own part as should entitle her to the milder glory appertaining to the good Rector's wife. All these hopes were now to be blotted out ignominiously. Defeat and retreat and failure were to be the conclusion of their first essay at life. "You are the best judge of what you ought to do," she said, with as much calmness as she could muster, but she could have dropped bitter tears upon the stocking she was mending if that would have done any good.

"I will do nothing without your consent," said the Rector. "Young Wentworth is going to stay in Carlingford. You need not look up so sharply, as if you were vexed to think *that* had anything to do with it. If he had not behaved like a fool, I never could have been led into such a mistake," said Mr Morgan, with indignation, taking a little walk to the other end of the room to refresh himself. "At the same time," said the Rector, severely, coming back after a pause, "to show any ill-feeling would be very unchristian either on your side or mine. If I were to accept Harry Scarsfield's offer, Proctor and I would do all we could to have young Wentworth appointed to Carlingford. There is nobody just now at All-Souls to take the living; and however much you may disapprove of him, my dear," said Mr Morgan, with increasing severity, "there is nothing that I know of to be said against him as a clergyman. If you can make up your mind to consent to it, and can see affairs in the same light as they appear to me, that is what I intend to do——"

Mrs Morgan's stocking had dropped on her knees as she listened; then it dropped on the floor, and she took no notice of it. When the Rector had finally delivered himself of his sentiments, which he did in the voice of a judge who was condemning some unfortunate to the utmost penalties of the law, his wife marked the conclusion of the sentence by a sob of strange excitement. She kept gazing at him for a few moments without feeling able to speak, and then she put down her face into her hands.

Words were too feeble to give utterance to her feelings at such a supreme moment. "Oh, William, I wonder if you ever can forgive me," sobbed the Rector's wife, with a depth of compunction which he, good man, was totally unprepared to meet, and knew no occasion for. He was even at the moment a little puzzled to have such a despairing petition addressed to him. "I hope so, my dear," he said, very sedately, as he came and sat down beside her, and could not refrain from uttering a little lecture upon temper, which fortunately Mrs Morgan was too much excited to pay any attention to. "It would be a great deal better if you did not give way to your feelings," said the Rector; "but in the mean time, my dear, it is your advice I want, for we must not take such a step unadvisedly," and he lifted up the stocking that had fallen, and contemplated, not without surprise, the emotion of his wife. The excellent man was as entirely unconscious that he was being put up again at that moment with acclamations upon his pedestal, as that he had at a former time been violently displaced from it, and thrown into the category of broken idols. All this would have been as Sanscrit to the Rector of Carlingford; and the only resource he had was to make in his own mind certain half-pitying, half-affectionate remarks upon the inexplicable weakness of women, and to pick up the stocking which his wife was darning, and finally to stroke her hair, which was still as pretty and soft and brown as it had been ten years ago. Under such circumstances a man does not object to feel himself on a platform of moral superiority. He even began to pet her a little, with a pleasant sense of forgiveness and forbearance. "You were perhaps a little cross, my love, but you don't think I am a man to be hard upon you," said the Rector. "Now you must dry your eyes and give me your advice—you know how much confidence I have always had in your advice——"

"Forgive me, William. I don't think there is any one so good as you are; and as long as we are together it does not matter to me where we are," said the repentant woman. But as she lifted up her head, her eye fell on the carpet, and a gleam of sudden delight passed through Mrs Morgan's mind. To be delivered from all her suspicions and injurious thoughts about her husband would have been a deliverance great enough for one day; but at the same happy moment to see a means of deliverance from the smaller as well as the greater cross of her existence seemed almost too good to be credible. She brightened up immediately when that thought occurred to her. "I think it is the very best thing you could do," she said. "We are both so fond of the country, and it is so much nicer to manage a country parish than a town one. We might have lived all our lives in Carlingford without knowing above half of the poor people," said Mrs Morgan, growing in warmth as she went on; "it is so different in a country parish. I never liked to say anything," she continued, with subtle feminine policy, "but I never—much—cared for Carlingford." She gave a sigh as she spoke, for she thought of the Virginian creeper and the five feet of new wall at that side of the garden, which had just been completed, to shut out the view of the train. Life does not contain any perfect pleasure. But when Mrs Morgan stooped to lift up some stray reels of cotton which the Rector's clumsy male fingers had dropped out of her workbox, her eye was again attracted by the gigantic roses and tulips on the carpet, and content and satisfaction filled her heart.

"I have felt the same thing, my dear," said Mr Morgan. "I don't say anything against Mr

Finial as an architect, but Scott himself could make nothing of such a hideous church. I don't suppose Wentworth will mind," said the Rector, with a curious sense of superiority. He felt his own magnanimous conduct at the moment almost as much as his wife had done, and could not help regarding Carlingford Church as the gift-horse which was not to be examined too closely in the mouth.

"No," said Mrs Morgan, not without a passing sensation of doubt on this point; "if he had only been frank and explained everything, there never could have been any mistake; but I am glad it has all happened," said the Rector's wife, with a little enthusiasm. "Oh, William, I have been such a wretch—I have been thinking—but now you are heaping coals of fire on his head," she cried, with a hysterical sound in her throat. It was no matter to her that she herself scarcely knew what she meant, and that the good Rector had not the faintest understanding of it. She was so glad, that it was almost necessary to be guilty of some extravagance by way of relieving her mind. "After all Mr Proctor's care in fitting the furniture, you would not, of course, think of removing it," said Mrs Morgan; "Mr Wentworth will take it as we did; and as for

Mrs Scarsfield, if you like her, William, you may be sure I shall," the penitent wife said softly, in the flutter and tremor of her agitation. As he saw himself reflected in her eyes, the Rector could not but feel himself a superior person, elevated over other men's shoulders. Such a sense of goodness promotes the amiability from which it springs. The Rector kissed his wife as he got up from his seat beside her, and once more smoothed down, with a touch which made her feel like a girl again, her pretty brown hair.

"That is all settled satisfactorily," said Mr Morgan, "and now I must go to my work again. I thought, if you approved of it, I would write at once to Scarsfield, and also to Buller of All-Souls."

"Do," said the Rector's wife—and she too bestowed, in her middle-aged way, a little caress, which was far from being unpleasant to the sober-minded man. He went down-stairs in a more agreeable frame of mind than he had known for a long time back. Not that he understood why she had cried about it when he laid his intentions before her. Had Mr Morgan been a Frenchman, he probably would have imagined his wife's heart to be touched by the graces of the Perpetual Curate; but being an Englishman, and rather more certain, on the whole, of her than of himself, it did not occur to him to speculate on the subject. He was quite able to content himself with the thought that women were incomprehensible, as he went back to his study. To be sure, it was best to understand them, if you could; but if not, it did not so very much matter, Mr Morgan thought; and in this pleasant condition of mind he went down-stairs and wrote a little sermon, which ever after was a great favourite, preached upon all special occasions, and always listened to with satisfaction, especially by the Rector's wife.

When Mrs Morgan was left alone she sat doing nothing for an entire half-hour, thinking of the strange and unhoped-for change that in a moment had occurred to her. Though she was not young, she had that sense of the grievousness, the unbearableness of trouble, which belongs to youth; for, after all, whatever female moralists may say on the subject, the patience of an unmarried woman wearing out her youth in the harassments of a long engagement, is something very different from the hard and many-sided experience of actual life. She had been accustomed for years to think that her troubles would be over when the long-expected event arrived; and when new and more vexatious troubles still sprang up after that event, the woman of one idea was not much better fitted to meet them than if she had been a girl. Now that the momentary cloud had been driven off, Mrs Morgan's heart rose more warmly than ever. She changed her mind in a moment about the All-Souls pudding, and even added, in her imagination, another dish to the dinner, without pausing to think that *that* also was much approved by Mr Leeson; and then her thoughts took another turn, and such a vision of a perfect carpet for a drawing-room—something softer and more exquisite than ever came out of mortal loom; full of repose and tranquillity, yet not without seducing beauties of design; a carpet which would never obtrude itself, but yet would catch the eye by dreamy moments in the summer twilight or over the winter fire—flashed upon the imagination of the Rector's wife. It would be sweet to have a house of one's own arranging, where everything would be in harmony; and though this sweetness was very secondary to the other satisfaction of having a husband who was not a clay idol, but really deserved his pedestal, it yet supplemented the larger delight, and rounded off all the corners of Mrs Morgan's present desires. She wished everybody as happy as herself, in the effusion of the moment, and thought of Lucy Wodehouse, with a little glow of friendliness in which there was still a tincture of admiring envy. All this that happy girl would have without the necessity of waiting for it; but then was it not the Rector, the rehabilitated husband, who would be the means of producing so much happiness? Mrs Morgan rose up as lightly as a girl when she had reached this stage, and opened her writing-desk, which was one of her wedding-presents, and too fine to be used on common occasions. She took out her prettiest paper, with her monogram in violet, which was her favourite colour. One of those kind impulses which are born of happiness moved her relieved spirit. To give to another the consolation of a brighter hope seemed at the moment the most natural way of expressing her own thankful feelings. Instead of going downstairs immediately to order dinner, she sat down instead at the table, and wrote the following note:—

"MY DEAR MR WENTWORTH,—I don't know whether you will think me a fair-weather friend seeking you only when everybody else is seeking you, and when you are no longer in want of support and sympathy. Perhaps you will exculpate me when you remember the last conversation we had; but what I write for at present is to ask if you would waive ceremony, and come to dinner with us to-night. I am aware that your family are still in Carlingford, and of course I don't know what engagements you may have; but if you are at liberty, pray come. If Mr Morgan and you had but known each other a little better, things could never have happened which have been a great grief and vexation to me; and I know the Rector *wishes very much* to have a little conversation with you, and has something to speak of in which you would be interested. Perhaps my husband might feel a little strange in asking you to overstep the barrier which somehow has been raised between you two; but I am sure if you knew each other better you would understand each other, and this is one of the things we women ought to be good for. I will take it as a proof that you consider me a friend if you accept my invitation. Our hour is half-past six.—Believe me, very sincerely, yours,

M. MORGAN."

When she had written this note Mrs Morgan went down-stairs, stopping at the library-door in passing. "I thought I might as well ask Mr Wentworth to come to us to-night, as we are to have some people to dinner," she said, looking in at the door. "I thought you might like to talk to him, William; and if his people are going away to-day, I daresay he will feel rather lonely to-night." Such was the Jesuitical aspect in which she represented the flag of truce she was sending. Mr Morgan was a little startled by action so prompt.

"I should like to hear from Buller first," said the Rector; "he might like to come to Carlingford himself, for anything I can tell; but, to be sure, it can do no harm to have Wentworth to dinner," said Mr Morgan, doubtfully; "only Buller, you know, might wish—and in that case it might not be worth our trouble to make any change."

In spite of herself, Mrs Morgan's countenance fell; her pretty scheme of poetic justice, her vision of tasteful and appropriate furniture, became obscured by a momentary mist. "At least it is only right to ask him to dinner," she said, in subdued tones, and went to speak to the cook in a frame of mind more like the common level of human satisfaction than that exultant and exalted strain to which she had risen at the first moment. Then she put on a black dress, and went to call on the Miss Wodehouses, who naturally came into her mind when she thought of the Perpetual Curate. As she went along Grange Lane she could not but observe a hackney cab, one of those which belonged to the railway station, lounging—if a cab could ever be said to lounge—in the direction of Wharfside. Its appearance specially attracted Mrs Morgan's attention in consequence of the apparition of Elsworthy's favourite errand-boy, who now and then poked his head furtively through the window, and seemed to be sitting in state inside. When she had gone a little farther she encountered Wodehouse and Jack Wentworth, who had just come from paying their visit to the sisters. The sight of these two revived her sympathies for the lonely women who had fallen so unexpectedly out of wealth into poverty; but yet she felt a little difficulty in framing her countenance to be partly sorrowful and partly congratulatory, as was necessary under these circumstances; for though she knew nothing of the accident which had happened that morning, when Lucy and the Perpetual Curate saw each other alone, she was aware of Miss Wodehouse's special position, and was sympathetic as became a woman who had "gone through" similar experiences. When she had got through her visit and was going home, it struck her with considerable surprise to see the cab still lingering about the corner of Prickett's Lane. Was Elsworthy's pet boy delivering his newspapers from that dignified elevation? or were they seizing the opportunity of conveying away the unfortunate little girl who had caused so much annoyance to everybody? When she went closer, with a little natural curiosity to see what else might be inside besides the furtive errand-boy, the cab made a little rush away from her, and the blinds were drawn down. Mrs Morgan smiled a little to herself with dignified calm. "As if it was anything to me!" she said to herself; and so went home to put out the dessert with her own hands. She even cut a few fronds of her favourite maidenhair to decorate the peaches, of which she could not help being a little proud. "I must speak to Mr Wentworth, if he comes, to keep on Thompson," she said to herself, and then gave a momentary sigh at thought of the new flue, which was as good as her own invention, and which it had cost her both time and money to arrange to her satisfaction. The peaches were lovely, but who could tell what they might be next year if a new Rector came who took no interest in the garden?—for Thompson, though he was a very good servant, required to be looked after, as indeed most good servants do. Mrs Morgan sighed a little when she thought of all her past exertions and the pains, of which she was scarcely yet beginning to reap the fruit. One man labours, and another enters into his labours. One thing, however, was a little consolatory, that she could take her ferns with her. But on the whole, after the first outburst of feeling, the idea of change, notwithstanding all its advantages, was in itself, like most human things, a doubtful pleasure. To be sure, it was only through its products that her feelings were interested about the new flue, whereas the drawing-room carpet was a standing grievance. When it was time to dress for dinner, the Rector's wife was not nearly so sure as before that she had never liked Carlingford. She began to forget the thoughts she had entertained about broken idols, and to remember a number of inconveniences attending a removal. Who would guarantee the safe transit of the china, not to speak of the *old* china, which was one of the most valuable decorations of the Rectory? This kind of breakage, if not more real, was at least likely to force itself more upon the senses than the other kind of fracture which this morning's explanation had happily averted; and altogether it was with mingled feeling that Mrs Morgan entered the drawing-room, and found it occupied by Mr Leeson, who always came too early, and who, on the present occasion, had some sufficiently strange news to tell.

CHAPTER XLVI.

MR WENTWORTH did not accept Mrs Morgan's sudden invitation, partly because his "people" did not leave Carlingford that evening, and partly because, though quite amiably disposed towards the Rector, whom he had worsted in fair fight, he was not sufficiently interested in anything he was like to hear or see in Mr Morgan's house to move him to spend his evening there. He returned a very civil answer to the invitation of the Rector's wife, thanking her warmly for her friendliness, and explaining that he could not leave his father on the last night of his stay in Carlingford; after which he went to dinner at his aunts', where the household was still much agitated. Not to speak of all the events which had happened and were happening, Jack, who had begun to tire of his new character of the repentant prodigal, had shown himself in a new light that evening, and was preparing to leave, to the relief of all parties. The prodigal, who no longer pretended to be penitent, had taken the conversation into his own hands at dinner. "I have had things my own way since I came here," said Jack; "somehow it appears I have a great luck for having things my own way. It is you scrupulous people who think of others and of such antiquated stuff as duty, and so forth, that get yourselves into difficulties. My dear aunt, I am going away; if I were to remain an inmate of this house—I mean to say, could I look forward to the privilege of continuing a member of this Christian family—another day, I should know better how to conduct myself; but I am going back to my bad courses, aunt Dora; I am returning to the world——"

"Oh! Jack, my dear, I hope not," said aunt Dora, who was much bewildered, and did not know what to say.

"Too true," said the relapsed sinner; "and considering all the lessons you have taught me, don't you think it is the best thing I could do? There is my brother Frank, who has been carrying other people about on his shoulders, and doing his duty; but I don't see that you good people are at all moved in his behalf. You leave him to fight his way by himself, and confer your benefits elsewhere, which is an odd sort of lesson for a worldling like me. As for Gerald, you know he's a virtuous fool, as I have heard you all declare. There is nothing in the world that I can see to prevent him keeping his living and doing as he pleases, as most parsons do. However, that's his own business. It is Frank's case which is the edifying case to me. If my convictions of sin had gone just a step farther," said the pitiless critic, "if I had devoted myself to bringing others to repentance, as is the first duty of a reformed sinner, my aunt Leonora would not have hesitated to give Skelmersdale to me——"

"Jack, hold your tongue," said Miss Leonora; but though her cheeks burned, her voice was not so firm as usual, and she actually failed in putting down the man who had determined to have his say.

"Fact, my dear aunt," said Jack: "if I had been a greater rascal than I am, and gone a little farther, you and your people would have thought me quite fit for a cure of souls. I'd have come in for your good things that way as well as other ways; but here is Frank, who even I can see is a right sort of parson. I don't pretend to fixed theological opinions," said this unlooked-for oracle, with a comic glance aside at Gerald, the most unlikely person present to make any response; "but, so far as I can see, he's a kind of fellow most men would be glad to make a friend of when they were under a cloud—not that he was ever very civil to me. I tell you, so far from rewarding him for being of the true sort, you do nothing but snub him, that I can see. He looks to me as good for work as any man I know; but you'll give your livings to any kind of wretched make-believe before you'll give them to Frank. I am aware," said the heir of the Wentworths, with a momentary flush, "that I have never been considered much of a credit to the family; but if I were to announce my intention of marrying and settling, there is not one of the name that would not lend a hand to smooth matters. That is the reward of wickedness," said Jack, with a laugh; "as for Frank, he's a perpetual curate, and may marry perhaps fifty years hence; that's the way you good people treat a man who never did anything to be ashamed of in his life; and you expect me to give up my evil courses after such a lesson? I trust I am not such a fool," said the relapsed prodigal. He sat looking at them all in his easy way, enjoying the confusion, the indignation, and wrath with which his address was received. "The man who gets his own way is the man who takes it," he concluded, with his usual composure, pouring out Miss Leonora's glass of claret as he spoke.

Nobody had ever before seen the strong-minded woman in so much agitation. "Frank knows what my feelings are," she said, abruptly. "I have a great respect for himself, but I have no confidence in his principles. I —I have explained my ideas about Church patronage——"

But here the Squire broke in. "I always said, sir," said the old man, with an unsteady voice, "that if I ever lived to see a thing or two amended that was undoubtedly objectionable, your brother Jack's advice would be invaluable to the family as a—as a man of the world. I have nothing to say against clergymen, sir," continued the Squire, without it being apparent whom he was addressing, "but I have always expressed my conviction of — of the value of your brother Jack's advice as—as a man of the world."

This speech had a wonderful effect upon the

assembled family, but most of all upon the son thus commended, who lost all his ease and composure as his father spoke, and turned his head stiffly to one side, as if afraid to meet the Squire's eyes, which indeed were not seeking his, but were fixed upon the table, as was natural, considering the state of emotion in which Mr Wentworth was. As for Jack, when he had steadied himself a little, he got up from his seat and tried to laugh, though the effort was far from being a successful one.

"Even my father applauds me, you see, because I am a scamp and don't deserve it," he said, with a voice which was partially choked. "Good-bye, sir; I am going away."

The Squire rose too, with the hazy bewildered look of which his other children were afraid.

"Good-bye, sir," said the old man, and then made a pause before he held out his hand. "You'll not forget what I've said, Jack," he added, with a little haste. "It's true enough, though I haven't that confidence in you that—that I might have had. I am getting old, and I have had two attacks, sir," said Mr Wentworth, with dignity; "and anyhow, I can't live for ever. Your brothers can make their own way in the world, but I haven't saved all that

I could have wished. When I am gone, Jack, be just to the girls and the little children," said the Squire; and with that took his son's hand and grasped it hard, and looked his heir full in the face.

Jack Wentworth was not prepared for any such appeal; he was still less prepared to discover the unexpected and inevitable sequence with which one good sentiment leads to another. He quite faltered and broke down in this unlooked-for emergency. "Father," he said unawares, for the first time for ten years, "if you wish it, I will join you in breaking the entail."

"No such thing, sir," said the Squire, who, so far from being pleased, was irritated and disturbed by the proposal. "I ask you to do your duty, sir, and not to shirk it," the head of the house said, with natural vehemence, as he stood with that circle of Wentworths round him, giving forth his code of honour to his unworthy heir.

While his father was speaking, Jack recovered a little from his momentary *attendrissement*. "Good-bye, sir—I hope you'll live a hundred years," he said, wringing his father's hand, "if you don't last out half-a-dozen of me, as you ought to do. But I'd rather not anticipate such a change. In that case," the prodigal went on with a certain huskiness in his voice, "I daresay I should not turn out so great a rascal as—as I ought to do. To-day and yesterday it has even occurred to me by moments that I was your son, sir," said Jack Wentworth; and then he made an abrupt stop and dropped the Squire's hand, and came to himself in a surprising way. When he turned towards the rest of the family, he was in perfect possession of his usual courtesy and good spirits. He nodded to them all round—with superb good-humour. "Good-bye, all of you; I wish you better luck, Frank, and not so much virtue. Perhaps you will have a better chance now the lost sheep has gone back to the wilderness. Good-bye to you all. I don't think I've any other last words to say." He lighted his cigar with his ordinary composure in the hall, and whistled one of his favourite airs as he went through the garden. "Oddly enough, however, our friend Wodehouse can beat me in that," he said, with a smile, to Frank, who had followed him out, "perhaps in other things too, who knows? Good-bye, and good-luck, old fellow." And thus the heir of the Wentworths disappeared into the darkness which swallowed him up, and was seen no more.

But naturally there was a good deal of commotion in the house. Miss Leonora, who never had known what it was to have nerves in the entire course of her existence, retired to her own room with a headache, to the entire consternation of the family. She had been a strong-minded woman all her life, and managed everybody's affairs without being distracted and hampered in her career by those doubts of her own wisdom, and questions as to her own motives, which will now and then afflict the minds of weaker people when they have to decide for others. But this time an utterly novel and unexpected accident had befallen Miss Leonora; a man of no principles at all had delivered his opinion upon her conduct—and so far from finding his criticism contemptible, or discovering in it the ordinary outcry of the wicked against the righteous, she had found it true, and by means of it had for perhaps the first time in her life seen herself as others saw her. Neither was the position in which she found herself one from which she could get extricated even by any daring arbitrary exertion of will, such as a woman in difficulties is sometimes capable of. To be sure, she might still have cut the knot in a summary feminine way;

might have said "No" abruptly to Julia Trench and her curate, and, after all, have bestowed Skelmersdale, like any other prize or reward of virtue, upon her nephew Frank—a step which Miss Dora Wentworth would have concluded upon at once without any hesitation. The elder sister, however, was gifted with a truer perception of affairs. Miss Leonora knew that there were some things which could be done, and yet could not be done—a piece of knowledge difficult to a woman. She recognised the fact that she had committed herself, and got into a corner from which there was but one possible egress; and as she acknowledged this to herself, she saw at the same time that Julia Trench (for whom she had been used to entertain a good-humoured contempt as a clever sort of girl enough) had managed matters very cleverly, and that, instead of dispensing her piece of patronage like an optimist to the best, she had, in fact, given it up to the most skilful and persevering angler, as any other woman might have done. The blow was bitter, and Miss Leonora did not seek to hide it from herself, not to say that the unpleasant discovery was aggravated by having been thus pointed out by Jack, who in his own person had taken her in, and cheated his sensible aunt. She felt humbled, and wounded in the tenderest point, to think that her reprobate nephew had seen through her, but that she had not been able to see through him, and had been deceived by his professions of penitence. The more she turned it over in her mind, the more Miss Leonora's head ached; for was it not growing apparent that she, who prided herself so much on her impartial judgment, had been moved, not by heroic and stoical justice and the love of souls, but a good deal by prejudice and a good deal by skilful artifice, and very little indeed by that highest motive which she called the glory of God? And it was Jack who had set all this before her clear as daylight. No wonder the excellent woman was disconcerted. She went to bed gloomily with her headache, and would tolerate no ministrations, neither of sal-volatile nor eau-de-cologne, nor even of green tea. "It always does Miss Dora a power of good," said the faithful domestic who made this last suggestion; but Miss Leonora answered only by turning the unlucky speaker out of the room, and locking the door against any fresh intrusion. Miss Dora's innocent headaches were articles of a very different kind from this, which proceeded neither from the heart nor the digestion, but from the conscience, as Miss Leonora thought—with, possibly, a little aid from the temper, though she was less conscious of that. It was indeed a long series of doubts and qualms, and much internal conflict, which resulted through the rapidly-maturing influences of mortification and humbled self-regard, in this ominous and awe-inspiring Headache which startled the entire assembled family, and added fresh importance to the general crisis of Wentworth affairs.

"I should not wonder if it was the Wentworth complaint," said Miss Dora, with a sob of fright, to the renewed and increased indignation of the Squire.

"I have already told you that the Wentworth complaint never attacks females," Mr Wentworth said emphatically, glad to employ what sounded like a contemptuous title for the inferior sex.

"Yes, oh yes; but then Leonora is not exactly what you would call—a female," said poor Miss Dora, from whom an emergency so unexpected had taken all her little wits.

While the house was in such an agitated condition, it is not to be supposed that it could be very comfortable for the gentlemen when they came up-stairs to the drawing-room, and found domestic sovereignty overthrown by a headache which nobody could comprehend, and chaos reigning in Miss Leonora's place. Naturally there was, for one of the party at least, a refuge sweet and close at hand, to which his thoughts had escaped already. Frank Wentworth did not hesitate to follow his thoughts. Against the long years when family bonds make up all that is happiest in life, there must always be reckoned those moments of agitation and revolution, during which the bosom of a family is the most unrestful and disturbing place in existence, from which it is well to have a personal refuge and means of escape. The Perpetual Curate gave himself a little shake, and drew a long breath, as he emerged from one green door in Grange Lane and betook himself to another. He shook himself clear of all the Wentworth perplexities, all the family difficulties and doubts, and betook himself into the paradise which was altogether his own, and where there were no conflicting interests or differences of opinion. He was in such a hurry to get there that he did not pay any attention to the general aspect of Grange Lane, or to the gossips who were gathered round Elsworthy's door: all that belonged to a previous stage of existence. At present he was full of the grand discovery, boldly stated by his brother Jack—"The man who gets his own way is the man who *takes* it." It was not an elevated doctrine, or one that had hitherto commended itself specially to the mind of the Perpetual Curate; but he could not help thinking of his father's pathetic reliance upon Jack's advice as a man of the world, as he laid up in his mind the prodigal's maxim, and felt, with a little thrill of excitement, that he was about to act on it; from which manner of stating the case Mr Wentworth's friends will perceive that self-will had seized upon him in the worst form; for he was not going boldly up to the new resolution with his eyes open, but had resigned himself to the tide, which was gradually rising in one united flux of love, pride, impatience, sophistry, and inclination; which he watched with a certain passive content, knowing that the stormy current would carry him away.

Mr Wentworth, however, reckoned without his host, as is now and then the case with most men, Perpetual Curates included. He walked into the other drawing-room, which was occupied only by two ladies, where the lamp was burning softly on the little table in the corner, and the windows, half open, admitted the fragrant air, the perfumed breath, and stillness and faint inarticulate noises of the night. Since the visit of Wodehouse in the morning, which had driven Lucy into her first fit of passion, an indescribable change had come over the house, which had now returned to the possession of its former owners, and looked again like home. It was very quiet in the familiar room which Mr Wentworth knew so well, for it was only when excited by events "beyond their control," as Miss Wodehouse said, that the sisters could forget what had happened so lately—the loss which had made a revolution in their world. Miss Wodehouse, who for the first time in her life was busy, and had in hand a quantity of mysterious calculations and lists to make out, sat at the table in the centre of the room, with her desk open, and covered with long slips of paper. Perhaps it was to save her Rector trouble that the gentle woman gave herself so much labour; perhaps she liked putting down on paper all the things that were indispensable for the new establishment. At all events, she looked up only to give Mr Wentworth a smile and sisterly nod of welcome as he came in and made his way to the corner where Lucy sat, not unexpectant. Out of the disturbed atmosphere he had just left, the Perpetual Curate came softly to that familiar corner, feeling that he had suddenly reached his haven, and that Eden itself could not have possessed a sweeter peace. Lucy in her black dress, with traces of the exhaustion of nature in her face, which was the loveliest face in the world to Mr Wentworth, looked up and welcomed him with that look of satisfaction and content which is the highest compliment one human creature can pay to another. His presence rounded off all the corners of existence to Lucy for that moment at least, and made the world complete and full. He sat down beside her at her work-table with no further interruption to the *tête-à-tête* than the presence of the kind elder sister at the table, who was absorbed in her lists, and who, even had that pleasant business been wanting, was dear and familiar enough to both to make her spectatorship just the sweet restraint which endears such intercourse all the more. Thus the Perpetual Curate seated himself, feeling in some degree master of the position; and surely here, if nowhere else in the world, the young man was justified in expecting to have his own way.

"They have settled about their marriage," said Lucy, whose voice was sufficiently audible to be heard at the table, where Miss Wodehouse seized her pen hastily and plunged it into the ink, doing her best to appear unconscious, but failing sadly in the attempt. "Mr Proctor is going away directly to make everything ready, and the marriage is to be on the 15th of next month."

"And ours?" said Mr Wentworth, who had not as yet approached that subject. Lucy knew that this event must be far off, and was not agitated about it as yet; on the contrary, she met his look sympathetically and with deprecation after the first natural blush, and soothed him in her feminine way, patting softly with her pretty hand the sleeve of his coat.

"Nobody knows," said Lucy. "We must wait, and have patience. We have more time to spare than they have," she added, with a little laugh. "We must wait."

"I don't see the *must*," said the Perpetual Curate. "I have been thinking it all over since the morning. I see no reason why I should always have to give in, and wait; self-sacrifice is well enough when it can't be helped, but I don't see any reason for postponing my happiness indefinitely. Look here, Lucy. It appears to me at present that there are only two classes of people in the world—those who will wait and those who won't. I don't mean to enrol myself among the martyrs. The man who gets his own way is the man who takes it. I don't see any reason in the world for concluding that I *must* wait."

Lucy Wodehouse was a very good young woman, a devoted Anglican, and loyal to all her duties; but she had always been known to possess a spark of spirit, and this rebellious quality came to a sudden blaze at so unlooked-for a speech. "Mr Wentworth," said Lucy, looking the Curate in the face with a look which was equivalent to making him a low curtsy, "I understood there were two people to be consulted as to the must or must not;" and having entered this protest, she withdrew her chair a little farther off, and bestowed her attention absolutely upon the piece of needle-work in her hand.

If the ground had suddenly been cut away

underneath Frank Wentworth's feet, he could not have been more surprised; for, to tell the truth, it had not occurred to him to doubt that he himself was the final authority on this point, though, to be sure, it was part of the conventional etiquette that the lady should "fix the day." He sat gazing at her with so much surprise that for a minute or two he could say nothing. "Lucy, I am not going to have you put yourself on the other side," he said at last; "there is not to be any opposition between you and me."

"That is as it may be," said Lucy, who was not mollified. "You seem to have changed your sentiments altogether since the morning, and there is no change in the circumstances, at least that I can see."

"Yes, there is a great change," said the young man. "If I could have sacrificed myself in earnest and said nothing——"

"Which you were quite free to do," interrupted Lucy, who, having given way to temper once to-day, found in herself an alarming proclivity towards a repetition of the offence.

"Which I was quite free to do," said the Perpetual Curate, with a smile, "but could not, and did not, all the same. Things are altogether changed. Now, be as cross as you please, you belong to me, *Lucia mia.* To be sure, I have no money——"

"I was not thinking of that," said the young lady, under her breath.

"Of course one has to think about it," said Mr Wentworth; "but the question is, whether we shall be happier and better going on separate in our usual way, or making up our minds to give up something for the comfort of being together. Perhaps you will forgive me for taking *that* view of the question," said the Curate, with a little enthusiasm. "I have got tired of ascetic principles. I don't see why it must be best to deny myself and postpone myself to other things and other people. I begin to be of my brother Jack's opinion. The children of this world are wiser in their generation than the children of light. A man who will wait has to wait. Providence does not invariably reward him after he has been tried, as we used to suppose. I am willing to be a poor man because I can't help it; but I am not willing to wait and trust my happiness to the future when it is in my reach now," said the unreasonable young man, to whom it was of course as easy as it was to Lucy to change the position of his chair, and prevent the distance between them being increased. Perhaps he might have carried his point even at that moment, had not Miss Wodehouse, who had heard enough to alarm her, come forward hastily in a fright on the prudential side.

"I could not help hearing what you were saying," said the elder sister, "Oh, Mr Wentworth, I hope you don't mean to say that you can't trust Providence? I'm sure that is not Lucy's way of thinking. I would not mind, and I am sure she would not mind, beginning very quietly; but then you have nothing, next to nothing, neither of you. It might not matter, just at the first," said Miss Wodehouse, with serious looks; "but then—afterwards, you know," and a vision of a nursery flashed upon her mind as she spoke. "Clergymen always have such large families," she said half out before she was aware, and stopped, covered with confusion, not daring to look at Lucy to see what effect such a suggestion might have had upon her. "I mean," cried Miss Wodehouse, hurrying on to cover over her inadvertence if possible, "I have seen such cases; and a poor clergyman who has to think of the grocer's bill and the baker's bill instead of his parish and his duty—

there are some things you young people know a great deal better than I do, but you don't know how dreadful it is to see that."

Here Lucy, on her part, was touched on a tender point, and interposed. "For a man to be teased about bills," said the young housekeeper, with flushed cheeks and an averted countenance, "it must be not his poverty, but his—his wife's fault."

"Oh, Lucy, don't say so," cried Miss Wodehouse; "what is a poor woman to do, especially when she has no money of her own, as you wouldn't have? and then the struggling, and getting old before your time, and all the burdens——"

"Please don't say any more," said Lucy; "there was no intention on—on any side to drive things to a decision. As for me, I have not a high opinion of myself. I would not be the means of diminishing any one's comforts," said the spiteful young woman. "How can I be sure that I might not turn out a very poor compensation? We settled this morning how all that was to be, and I for one have not changed my mind—as yet," said Lucy. That was all the encouragement Mr Wentworth got when he propounded his new views. Things looked easy enough when he was alone, and suffered himself to drift on pleasantly on the changed and heightened current of personal desires and wishes; but it became apparent to him, after that evening's discussion, that even in Eden itself, though the dew had not yet dried on the leaves, it would be highly incautious for any man to conclude that he was sure of having his own way. The Perpetual Curate returned a sadder and a more doubtful man to Mrs Hadwin's, to his own apartments; possibly, as the two states of mind so often go together, a wiser individual too.

CHAPTER XLVII.

The dinner-party at the Rectory, to which Mr Wentworth did not go, was much less interesting and agreeable than it might have been had he been present. As for the Rector and his wife, they could not but feel themselves in a somewhat strange position, having between them a secret unsuspected by the company. It was difficult to refrain from showing a certain flagging of interest in the question of the church restoration, about which, to be sure, Mr Finial was just as much concerned as he had been yesterday; though Mr Morgan, and even Mrs Morgan, had suffered a great and unexplainable diminution of enthusiasm. And then Mr Leeson, who was quite unaware of the turn that affairs had taken, and who was much too obtuse to understand how the Rector could be anything but exasperated against the Perpetual Curate by the failure of the investigation, did all that he could to make himself disagreeable, which was saying a good deal. When Mrs Morgan came into the drawing-room, and found this obnoxious individual occupying the most comfortable easy-chair, and turning over at his ease the great book of ferns, nature-printed, which was the pet decoration of the table, her feelings may be conceived by any lady who has gone through a similar trial; for Mr Leeson's hands were not of the irreproachable purity which becomes the fingers of a gentleman when he goes out to dinner. "I know some people who always wear gloves when they turn over a portfolio of prints," Mrs Morgan said, coming to the Curate's side to protect her book if possible, "and these require quite as much care;" and she had to endure a discussion upon the subject, which was still more trying to her feelings, for Mr Leeson pretended to know about ferns on the score of having a Wardian case in his lodgings (which belonged to his landlady), though in reality he could scarcely tell the commonest spleenwort from a lycopodium. While Mrs Morgan went through this trial, it is not to be wondered at if she hugged to her heart the new idea of leaving Carlingford, and thought to herself that whatever might be the character of the curate (if there was one) at Scarsfield, any change from Mr Leeson must be for the better. And then the unfortunate man, as if he was not disagreeable enough already, began to entertain his unwilling hostess with the latest news.

"There is quite a commotion in Grange Lane," said Mr Leeson. "Such constant disturbances must deteriorate the property, you know. Of course, whatever one's opinion may be, one must keep it to one's self, after the result of the investigation; though I can't say *I* have unbounded confidence in trial by jury," said the disagreeable young man.

"I am afraid I am very slow of comprehension," said the Rector's wife. "I don't know in the least what you mean about trial by jury. Perhaps it would be best to put the book back on the table; it is too heavy for you to hold."

"Oh, it doesn't matter," said Mr Leeson—"I mean about Wentworth, of course. When a man is popular in society, people prefer to shut their eyes. I suppose the matter is settled for the present, but you and I know better than to believe——"

"I beg you will speak for yourself, Mr Leeson," said Mrs Morgan, with dignity. "I have always had the highest respect for Mr Wentworth."

"Oh, I beg your pardon," said the disagreeable Curate. "I forgot; almost all the ladies are on Mr Wentworth's side. It appears that little girl of Elsworthy's has disappeared again; that was all I was going to say."

And, fortunately for the Curate, Colonel Chiley, who entered the room at the moment, diverted from him the attention of the lady of the house; and after that there was no opportunity of broaching the subject again until dinner was almost over. Then it was perhaps the All-Souls pudding that warmed Mr Leeson's soul; perhaps he had taken a little more wine than usual. He took sudden advantage of that curious little pause which occurs at a well-conducted dinner-table, when the meal is concluded, and the fruit (considered apparently, in orthodox circles, a paradisaical kind of food which needs no blessing) alone remains to be discussed. As soon as the murmur of thanks from the foot of the table was over, the Curate incautiously rushed in before anybody else could break silence, and delivered his latest information at a high pitch of voice.

"Has any one heard about the Elsworthys?" said Mr Leeson; "something fresh has happened there. I hope your verdict yesterday will not be called in question. The fact is, I believe that the girl has been taken away again. They say she has gone and left a letter saying that she is to be made a lady of. I don't know what we are to understand by that. There was some private service or other going on at St Roque's very early in the morning. Marriage is a sacrament, you know. Perhaps Mr Wentworth or his brother——"

"They are a queer family, the Wentworths," said old Mr Western, "and such lots of them, sir—such lots of them. The old ladies seem to have settled down here. I am not of their way of thinking, you know, but they're very good to the poor."

"Mr Frank Wentworth is going to succeed his brother, I suppose," said Mr Leeson; "it is very lucky for a man who gets himself talked of to have a family living to fall back upon——"

"No such thing—no such thing," said Mr Proctor, hastily. "Mr Frank Wentworth means to stay here."

"Dear me!" said the disagreeable Curate,

with an elaborate pause of astonishment. "Things must be bad indeed," added that interesting youth, with solemnity, shaking the devoted head, upon which he did not know that Mrs Morgan had fixed her eyes, "if his own family give him up, and leave him to starve here. They never would give him up if they had not very good cause. Oh, come; I shouldn't like to believe that! *I* know how much a curate has to live on," said Mr Leeson, with a smile of engaging candour. "Before they give him .up like that, with two livings in the family, they must have very good cause."

"Very good cause indeed," said Mrs Morgan, from the head of the table. The company in general had, to tell the truth, been a little taken aback by the Curate's observations; and there was almost the entire length of the table between the unhappy man and the Avenger. "So good a reason, that it is strange how it should not have occurred to a brother clergyman. That is the evil of a large parish," said the Rector's wife, with beautiful simplicity; "however hard one works, one never can know above half of the poor people; and I suppose you have been occupied in the other districts, and have not heard what a great work Mr Wentworth is doing. I have reason to know," said Mrs Morgan, with considerable state, "that he will remain in Carlingford in a very different position from that which he has filled hitherto. Mr Leeson knows how much a curate has to live upon, but I am afraid that is all he does know of such a life as Mr Wentworth's." Mrs Morgan paused for a moment to get breath, for her excitement was considerable, and she had many wrongs to avenge. "There is a great deal of difference in curates, as well as in other things," said the indignant woman. "I have reason to know that Mr Wentworth will remain in Carlingford in quite a different position. Now and then, even in this world, things come right like a fairy tale—that is, when the authority is in the right hands;" the Rector's wife went on, with a smile at her husband, which disarmed that astonished man. "Perhaps if Mr Leeson had the same inducement as Mr Wentworth, he too would make up his mind to remain in Carlingford." Mrs Morgan got up, as she made this speech, with a rustle and sweep of drapery which seemed all addressed to the unhappy Curate, who stumbled upon his feet like the other gentlemen, but dared not for his life have approached her to open the door. Mr Leeson felt that he had received his *congé*, as he sank back into his chair. He was too much stunned to speculate on the subject, or ask himself what was going to happen. Whatever was going to happen, there was an end of *him*. He had eaten the last All-Souls pudding that he ever would have presented to him under *that* roof. He sank back in the depths of despair upon his seat, and suffered the claret to pass him in the agony of his feelings. Mr Wentworth and Mrs Morgan were avenged.

This was how it came to be noised abroad in Carlingford that some great change of a highly favourable character was about to occur in the circumstances and position of the Curate of St Roque's. It was discussed next day throughout the town, as soon as people had taken breath after telling each other about Rosa Elsworthy, who had indisputably been carried off from her uncle's house on the previous night. When the Wentworth family were at dinner, and just as the board was being spread in the Rectory, where Mrs Morgan was half an hour later than usual, having company, it had been discovered in Elsworthy's that the prison was vacant, and the poor little bird had flown. Mr Wentworth was aware of a tumult about the shop when he went to the Miss Wodehouses, but was preoccupied, and paid no attention; but Mr Leeson, who was not preoccupied, had already heard all about it when he entered the Rectory. That day it was all over the town, as may be supposed. The poor, little, wicked, unfortunate creature had disappeared, no one knew how, at the moment, apparently, when Elsworthy went to the railway for the evening papers, a time when the errand-boys were generally rampant in the well-conducted shop. Mrs Elsworthy, for her part, had seized that moment to relieve her soul by confiding to Mrs Hayles next door how she was worrited to death with one thing and another, and did not expect to be alive to tell the tale if things went on like this for another month; but that Elsworthy was infatuated like, and wouldn't send the hussy away, his wife complained to her sympathetic neighbour. When Elsworthy came back, however, he was struck by the silence in the house, and sent the reluctant woman up-stairs—"To see if she's been and made away with herself, I suppose," the indignant wife said, as she obeyed, leaving Mrs Hayles full of curiosity on the steps of the door. Mrs Elsworthy, however, uttered a great shriek a moment after, and came down, with a frightened face, carrying a large pincushion, upon which, skewered through and through with the biggest pin she could find, Rosa had deposited her letter of leave-taking. This important document was read over in the shop by an ever-increasing group, as the news got abroad—for Elsworthy, like his wife, lost his head, and rushed about hither and thither, asking wild questions as to who had seen her last. Perhaps, at the bottom, he was not so desperate as he looked, but was rather grateful than angry with Rosa for solving the difficulty. This is what the poor little runaway said—

"Dear Uncle and Aunt,—I write a line to let you know that them as can do better for me than any belonging to me has took me away for good. Don't make no reflections, please, nor blame nobody; for I never could have done no good, nor had any 'appiness at Carlingford after all as has happened. I don't bear no grudge, though aunt has been so unkind; but I forgive her, and uncle also. My love to all friends; and you may tell Bob Hayles as I won't forget him, but will order all my physic regular at his father's shop.—Your affectionate niece,

"ROSA.

"*P.S.*—Uncle has no occasion to mind, for them as has took charge of me has promised to make a lady of me, as he always said I was worthy of; and I leave all my things for aunt's relations, as I can't wear such poor clothes in my new station of life."

Such was the girl's letter, with its natural impertinences and natural touch of kindness; and it made a great commotion in the neighbourhood, where a few spasmodic search-parties were made up with no real intentions, and came to nothing, as was to be expected. It was a dreadful thing, to be sure, to happen to a respectable family; but when things had gone so far, the neighbours, on the whole, were inclined to believe it was the best thing Rosa could have done; and the Elsworthys, husband and wife, were concluded to be of the same opinion. When Carlingford had exhausted this subject, and had duly discussed the probabilities as to where she had gone, and whether Rosa could be the lady in a veil who had been handed into the express night-train by two gentlemen, of whom a railway-porter bore cautious testimony, the other mysterious rumour about Mr Wentworth had its share of popular attention. It was discussed in Masters's with a solemnity becoming the occasion, everybody being convinced of the fact, and nobody knowing how it was to be. One prevailing idea was, that Mr Wentworth's brother, who had succeeded to his mother's fortune (which was partially true, like most popular versions of family history, his mother's fortune being now Gerald's sole dependence), intended to establish a great brotherhood, upon the Claydon model, in Carlingford, of which the Perpetual Curate was to be the head. This idea pleased the imagination of the town, which already saw itself talked of in all the papers, and anticipated with excitement the sight of English brothers of St Benedict walking about in the streets, and people from the 'Illustrated News' making drawings of Grange Lane. To be sure, Gerald Wentworth had gone over to the Church of Rome, which was a step too far to be compatible with the English brotherhood; but popular imagination, when puzzled and in a hurry, does not take time to master all details. Then, again, opinion wavered, and it was supposed to be the Miss Wentworths who were the agents of the coming prosperity. They had made up their mind to endow St Roque's, and apply to the Ecclesiastical Commissioners to have it erected into a parochial district, rumour reported; and the senior assistant in Masters's, who was suspected of Low-Church tendencies, was known to be a supporter of this theory. Other ideas of a vaguer character floated through the town, of which no one could give any explanation; but Carlingford was unanimous in the conviction that good fortune was coming somehow to the popular favourite, who a week ago had occupied temporarily the position of the popular *bête noire* and impersonation of evil. "But the real sort always triumphs at the last," was the verdict of Wharfside, which, like every primitive community, believed in poetic justice; and among the bargemen and their wives much greater elevation than that of a district church or the headship of a brotherhood was expected for "the clergyman." If the Queen had sent for him immediately, and conferred upon him a bishopric, or at least appointed him her private chaplain, such a favour would have excited no surprise in Wharfside, where indeed the public mind was inclined to the opinion that the real use of queens and other such dignitaries was to find out and reward merit. Mr Wentworth himself laughed when the gossip reached his ears. "My people have given away all they had to give," he said to somebody who asked the question; "and I know no prospect I have of being anything but a Perpetual Curate, unless the Queen sends for me and appoints me to a bishopric, as I understand is expected in Prickett's Lane. If I come to any advancement," said the Curate of St Roque's, "it must be in social estimation, and not in worldly wealth, which is out of my way;" and he went down to Wharfside rather cheerfully than otherwise, having begun to experience that pertinacity carries the day, and that it might be possible to goad Lucy into the experiment of how much her housekeeping talents were good for, and whether, with a good wife, even a Perpetual Curate might be able to live without any particular bother in respect to the grocer's bill. Mr Wentworth being at present warmly engaged in this business of persuasion, and as intent as ever on having his own way, was not much affected by the Carlingford gossip. He went his way to Wharfside all the same, where the service was conducted as of old, and where all the humble uncertain voices were buoyed up and carried on by the steady pure volume of liquid sound which issued from Lucy Wodehouse's lips into the utterance of such a Magnificat as filled Mr Wentworth's mind with exultation. It was the woman's part in the worship—independent, yet in a sweet subordination; and the two had come back—though with the difference that their love was now avowed and certain, and they were known to belong to each other—to much the same state of feeling in which they were before the Miss Wentworths came to Carlingford, or anything uncomfortable had happened. They had learned various little lessons, to be sure, in the interim, but experience had not done much more for them than it does for ordinary human creatures, and the chances are that Mr Wentworth would have conducted himself exactly in the same manner another time had he been placed in similar circumstances; for the lessons of experience, however valuable, are sometimes very slow of impressing themselves upon a generous and hasty temperament, which has high ideas of honour and consistency, and rather piques itself on a contempt for self-interest and external advantages—which was the weakness of the

Curate of St Roque's. He returned to the "great work" in Wharfside with undiminished belief in it, and a sense of being able to serve his God and his fellow-creatures, which, though it may seem strange to some people, was a wonderful compensation to him for the loss of Skelmersdale. "After all, I doubt very much whether, under any circumstances, we could have left such a work as is going on here," he said to Lucy as they came up Prickett's Lane together, where the poor woman had just died peaceably in No. 10, and got done with it, poor soul; and the Sister of Mercy, in her grey cloak, lifted towards him the blue eyes which were full of tears, and answered with natural emphasis, "Impossible! it would have been deserting our post," and drew a step closer to him in the twilight with a sense of the sweetness of that plural pronoun which mingled so with the higher sense that it was impossible to disjoin them. And the two went on under the influence of these combined sentiments, taking comfort out of the very hardness of the world around them, in which their ministrations were so much needed, and feeling an exaltation in the "duty," which was not for one, but for both, and a belief in the possibility of mending matters, in which their love for each other bore a large share; for it was not in human nature thus to begin the ideal existence, without believing in its universal extension, and in the amelioration of life and the world.

"That is all they think of," said poor Miss Wodehouse, who, between her wondering inspection of the two "young people" and her own moderate and sensible love-affairs, and the directions which it was necessary to give to her Rector about the furnishing of the new house, was more constantly occupied than she had ever been in her life; "but then, if they marry, what are they to live upon? and if they don't marry——"

"Perhaps something will turn up, my dear," said old Mrs Western, who had an idea that Providence was bound to provide for two good young people who wanted to marry; and thus the two ladies were forced to leave the matter, where, indeed, the historian of events in Carlingford would willingly leave it also, not having much faith in the rewards of virtue which come convenient in such an emergency. But it is only pure fiction which can keep true to nature, and weave its narrative in analogy with the ordinary course of life—whereas history demands exactness in matters of *fact*, which are seldom true to nature, or amenable to any general rule of existence.

Before proceeding, however, to the narrative of the unexpected advancement and promotion which awaited the Perpetual Curate, it may be as well to notice that the Miss Wentworths, who during the summer had kindly given their house at Skelmersdale to some friends who had returned in the spring from India, found themselves now in a position to return to their own proper dwelling-place, and made preparations accordingly for leaving Carlingford, in which, indeed, they had no further occupation; for, to be sure, except to the extent of that respect which a man owes to his aunts, they had no special claim upon Frank Wentworth, or right to supervise his actions, save on account of Skelmersdale, which was now finally disposed of and given away. It cannot be said that Miss Leonora had ever fully recovered the remarkable indisposition which her nephew Jack's final address had brought upon her. The very next morning she fulfilled her pledges as a woman of honour, and bestowed Skelmersdale positively and finally upon Julia Trench's curate, who indeed made a creditable enough rector in his way; but after she had accomplished this act, Miss Leonora relapsed into one unceasing watch upon her nephew Frank, which was far from dispelling the tendency to headache which she showed at this period for the first and only time in her life. She watched him with a certain feeling of expiation, as she might have resorted to self-flagellation had she lived a few hundred years before, and perhaps suffered more acute pangs in that act of discipline than could be inflicted by any physical scourge. The longer she studied the matter the more thoroughly was Miss Leonora convinced not only that the Perpetual Curate was bent on doing his duty, but that he *did* it with all the force of high faculties, and a mind much more thoroughly trained, and of finer material than was possessed by the man whom she had made rector of Skelmersdale. The strong-minded woman bore quietly, with a kind of defiance, the sharp wounds with which her self-esteem was pierced by this sight. She followed up her discovery, and made herself more and more certain of the mistake she had made, not sparing herself any part of her punishment. As she pursued her investigations, too, Miss Leonora became increasingly sensible that it was not his mother's family whom he resembled, as she had once thought, but that he was out and out a Wentworth, possessed of all the family features; and this was the man whom by her own act she had disinherited of his natural share in the patronage of the family, substituting for her own flesh and blood an individual for whom, to tell the truth, she had little respect! Perhaps if she had been able to sustain herself with the thought that it was entirely a question of "principle," the retrospect might not have been so hard upon Miss Leonora; but being a woman of very distinct and uncompromising vision, she could not conceal from herself either Julia Trench's cleverness or her own mixed and doubtful motives. Having this sense of wrong and injustice, and general failure of the duty of kindred towards Frank, it might have been supposed a little comfort to Miss Leonora to perceive that he had entirely recovered from his disappointment, and was no longer in her power, if indeed he had ever been so. But the fact was, that if anything could have aggravated her personal smart, it would have been the fact of Frank's indifference and cheerfulness, and evident capability of contenting himself with his duty and his favourite district, and his Lucy—whom, to be sure, he could not marry, being only a Perpetual Curate. The spectacle came to have a certain fascination for Miss Wentworth. She kept watching him with a grim satisfaction, punishing herself, and at the same time comforting herself with the idea that, light as he made of it, he must be suffering too. She could not bear to think that he had escaped clean out of her hands, and that the decision she had come to, which produced so much pain to herself, was innoxious to Frank; and at the same time, though she could not tolerate his composure, and would have preferred to see him angry and revengeful, his evident recovery of spirits and general exhilaration increased Miss Leonora's respect for the man she had wronged. In this condition of mind the strong-minded aunt lingered over her preparations for removal, scorning much the rumour in Carlingford about her nephew's advancement, and feeling that she could never forgive him if by any chance promotion should come to him after all. "He will stay where he is. He will be a perpetual curate," Miss Leonora said, uttering what was in reality a hope under the shape of a taunt; and things were still in this position when Grange Lane in general and Miss Dora in particular (from the window of the summer-house) were startled much by the sight of the Rector, in terribly correct clerical costume, as if he were going to dine with the bishop, who walked slowly down the road like a man charged with a mission, and, knocking at Mrs Hadwin's door, was admitted immediately to a private conference with the Curate of St Roque's.

CHAPTER XLVIII.

It was the same afternoon that Mr Wentworth failed to attend, as he had never been known to fail before, at the afternoon's school which he had set up in Prickett's Lane for the young bargemen, who between the intervals of their voyages had a little leisure at that hour of the day. It is true there was a master provided, and the presence of the Perpetual Curate was not indispensable; but the lads, among whom, indeed, there were some men, were so much used to his presence as to get restless at their work on this unprecedented emergency. The master knew no other resource than to send for Miss Lucy Wodehouse, who was known to be on the other side of Prickett's Lane at the moment, superintending a similar educational undertaking for the benefit of the girls. It was, as may be supposed, embarrassing to Lucy to be called upon to render an account of Mr Wentworth's absence, and invited to take his place in this public and open manner; but then the conventional reticences were unknown in Wharfside, and nobody thought it necessary to conceal his certainty that the Curate's movements were better known to Lucy than to anybody else. She had to make answer with as much composure as possible in the full gaze of so many pair of curious eyes, that she did not know why Mr Wentworth was absent—"Somebody is sick, perhaps," said Lucy, repeating an excuse which had been made before for the Perpetual Curate; "but I hope it does not make any difference," she went on, turning round upon all the upturned heads which were neglecting their work to stare at her. "Mr Wentworth would be grieved to think that his absence did his scholars any injury." Lucy looked one of the ringleaders in the eyes as she spoke, and brought him to his senses—all the more effectually, to be sure, because she knew all about him, and was a familiar figure to the boy, suggesting various little comforts, for which, in Prickett's Lane, people were not ungrateful. But when she went back again to her girls, the young lady found herself in a state of excitement which was half annoyance and half a kind of shy pleasure. To be sure, it was quite true that they did belong to each other; but at the same time, so long as she was Lucy Wodehouse, she had no right to be called upon to represent "the clergyman," even in the "district" which was so important to both. And then it occurred to her to remember that if she remained Lucy Wodehouse that was not the Curate's fault—from which thought she went on to reflect that going away with Mr and Mrs Proctor when they were married was not a charming prospect, not to say that it involved a renunciation of the district for the present at least, and possibly for ever; for if Mr Wentworth could not marry as long as he was a Perpetual Curate, it followed of necessity that he could not marry until he had left Carlingford—an idea which Lucy turned over in her mind very seriously as she walked home, for this once unattended. A new light seemed to be thrown upon the whole matter by this thought. To consent to be married simply for her own happiness, to the disadvantage in any respect of her husband, was an idea odious to this young woman, who, like most young women, preferred to represent even to herself that it was for *his* happiness that she permitted herself to be persuaded to marry; but if duty were involved, that was quite another affair. It was quite evident to Lucy, as she walked towards Grange Lane, that the Curate would not be able to find any one to take her place in the district; perhaps also—for she was honest even in her self-delusions — Lucy was aware that she might herself have objections to the finding of a substitute; and what then? Was the great work to be interrupted because she could not bear the idea of possibly diminishing some of his external comforts by allowing him to have his way, and to be what he considered happy? Such was the wonderful length to which her thoughts had come when she reached the garden door, from which Mr Wentworth himself, flushed and eager, came hastily out as she approached. So far from explaining his unaccountable absence, or even greeting her with ordinary politeness, the young man seized her by the arm and brought her into the garden with a rapidity which made her giddy. "What is it—what do you mean?" Lucy cried with amazement as she found herself whirled through the sunshine and half carried up the stairs. Mr Wentworth made no answer until he had deposited her breathless in her own chair, in her own corner, and then got down on his knee beside her, as men in his crazy circumstances are not unapt to do.

"Lucy, look here. I was a Perpetual Curate the other day when you said you would have me," said the energetic lover, who was certainly out of his wits, and did not know what he was saying—"and you said you did not mind?"

"I said it did not matter," said Lucy, who was slightly piqued that he did not recollect exactly the form of so important a decision. "I knew well enough you were a Perpetual Curate. Has anything happened, or are you going out of your mind?"

"I think it must be that," said Mr Wentworth. "Something so extraordinary has happened that I cannot believe it. Was I in Prickett's Lane this afternoon as usual, or was I at home in my own room talking to the Rector—or have I fallen asleep somewhere, and is the whole thing a dream?"

"You certainly were not in Prickett's Lane," said Lucy. "I see what it is. Miss Leonora Wentworth has changed her mind, and you are going to have Skelmersdale after all. I did not think you could have made up your mind to leave the district. It is not news that gives me any pleasure," said the Sister of Mercy, as she loosed slowly off from her shoulders the grey cloak which was the uniform of the district. Her own thoughts had been so different that she felt intensely mortified to think of the unnecessary decision she had been so near making, and disappointed that the offer of a living could have moved her lover to such a pitch of pleasure. "All men are alike, it seems," she said to herself, with a little quiver in her lip—a mode of forestalling his communications which filled the Perpetual Curate with amazement and dismay.

"What are you thinking of?" he said. "Miss Leonora Wentworth has not changed her mind. That would have been a natural accident enough, but this is incredible. If you like, Lucy," he added, with an unsteady laugh, "and will consent to my original proposition, you may marry on the 15th, not the Perpetual Curate of St Roque's, but the Rector of Carlingford. Don't look at me with such an unbelieving countenance. It is quite true."

"I wonder how you can talk so," cried Lucy, indignantly; "it is all a made-up story; you know it is. I don't like practical jokes," she went on, trembling a little, and taking another furtive look at him—for somehow it was too wonderful not to be true.

"If I had been making up a story, I should have kept to what was likely," said Mr Wentworth. "The Rector has been with me all the afternoon—he says he has been offered his father's rectory, where he was brought up, and that he has made up his mind to accept it, as he always was fond of the country;—and that he has recommended me to his College for the living of Carlingford."

"Yes, yes," said Lucy, impatiently, "that is very good of Mr Morgan; but you know you are not a member of the College, and why should you have the living? I knew it could not be true."

"They are all a set of old —— Dons," said the Perpetual Curate; "that is, they are the most accomplished set of fellows in existence, Lucy—or at least they ought to be—but they are too superior to take an ordinary living, and condescend to ordinary existence. Here has Carlingford been twice vacant within a year—which is an unprecedented event—and Buller, the only man who would think of it, is hanging on for a colonial bishopric, where he can publish his book at his leisure. Buller is a great friend of Gerald's. It is incredible, *Lucia mia*, but it is true."

"Is it true? are you *sure* it is true?" cried Lucy; and in spite of herself she broke down and gave way, and let her head rest on the first convenient support it found, which turned out, naturally enough, to be Mr Wentworth's shoulder, and cried as if her heart was breaking. It is so seldom in this world that things come just when they are wanted; and this was not only an acceptable benefice, but implied the entire possession of the "district" and the most conclusive vindication of the Curate's honour. Lucy cried out of pride and happiness and glory in him. She said to herself, as Mrs Morgan had done at the beginning of her incumbency, "He will be such a Rector as Carlingford has never seen." Yet at the same time, apart from her glorying and her pride, a certain sense of pain, exquisite though shortlived, found expression in Lucy's tears. She had just been making up her mind to accept a share of his lowliness, and to show the world that even a Perpetual Curate, when his wife was equal to her position, might be poor without feeling any of the degradations of poverty; and now she was forestalled, and had nothing to do but accept his competence, which it would be no credit to manage well! Such were the thoughts to which she was reduced, though she had come home from Prickett's Lane persuading herself that it was duty only, and the wants of the district, which moved her. Lucy cried, although not much given to crying, chiefly because it was the only method she could find of giving expression to the feelings which were too varied and too complicated for words.

All Carlingford knew the truth about Mr Wentworth's advancement that evening, and on the next day, which was Sunday, the Church of St Roque's was as full as if the plague had broken out in Carlingford, and the population had rushed out, as they might have done in medieval times, to implore the succour of the physician-saint. The first indication of the unusual throng was conveyed to Mr Wentworth in his little vestry after the choristers had filed into the church in their white surplices, about which, to tell the truth, the Perpetual Curate was less interested than he had once been. Elsworthy, who had been humbly assisting the young priest to robe himself, ventured to break the silence when they were alone.

"The church is very full, sir," said Elsworthy; "there's a deal of people come, sir, after hearing the news. I don't say as I've always been as good a servant as I ought to have been; but it was all through being led away, and not knowing no better, and putting my trust where I shouldn't have put it. I've had a hard lesson, sir, and I've learnt better," he continued, with a sidelong glance at the Curate's face; "it was all a mistake."

"I was not finding fault with you, that I am aware of," said Mr Wentworth, with a little surprise.

"No, sir," said Elsworthy, "I'm aware as you wasn't finding no fault; but there's looks as speaks as strong as words, and I can feel as you haven't the confidence in me as you once had. I ain't ashamed to say it, sir," continued the clerk of St Roque's. "I'm one as trusted in that girl's innocent looks, and didn't believe as she could do no harm. She's led me into ill-feeling with my clergyman, sir, and done me a deal o' damage in my trade, and now she's gone off without as much as saying 'Thank you for your kindness.' It's a hard blow upon a man as was fond of her, and I didn't make no difference, no more than if she had been my own child."

"Well, well," said the Curate, "I daresay it was a trial to you; but you can't expect me to take much interest in it after all that has passed. Let bygones be bygones," said Mr Wentworth, with a smile, "as indeed you once proposed."

"Ah! sir, that was my mistake," sighed the penitent. "I would have 'umbled myself more becoming, if I had known all as I know now. You're a-going off to leave St Roque's, where we've all been so happy," said Mr Elsworthy, in pathetic tones. "I don't know as I ever was as 'appy, sir, as here, a-listening to them beautiful sermons, and a-giving my best attention to see as the responses was well spoke out, and things done proper. Afore our troubles began, sir, I don't know as I had a wish in the world, unless it was to see an 'andsome painted window in the chancel, which is all as is wanted to make the church perfect; and now you're a-going to leave, and nobody knows what kind of a gentleman may be sent. If you wouldn't think I was making too bold," said Elsworthy, "it ain't my opinion as you'll ever put up with poor old Norris as is in the church. Men like Mr Morgan and Mr Proctor as had no cultivation doesn't mind; but for a gentleman as goes through the service as you does it, Mr Wentworth——"

Mr Wentworth laughed, though he was fully robed and ready for the reading-desk, and knew that his congregation was waiting. He held his watch in his hand, though it already marked the half minute after eleven. "So you would like to be clerk in the parish church?" he said, with what seemed a quite unnecessary amount of amusement to the anxious functionary by his side.

"I think as you could never put up with old Norris, sir," said Elsworthy; "as for leading of the responses, there ain't such a thing done in Carlingford Church. I don't speak for myself," said the public-spirited clerk, "but it ain't a right thing for the rising generation; and it ain't everybody as would get into your way in a minute—for you have a way of your own, sir, in most things, and if you'll excuse me for saying of it, you're very particular. It ain't every man, sir, as could carry on clear through the service along of you, Mr Wentworth; and you wouldn't put up with old Norris, not for a day."

Such was the conversation which opened this memorable Sunday to Mr Wentworth. Opposite to him, again occupying the seat where his wife should have been, had he possessed one, were the three Miss Wentworths, his respected aunts, to whose opinion, however, the Curate did not feel himself bound to defer very greatly in present circumstances; and a large and curious congregation ranged behind them, almost as much concerned to see how Mr Wentworth would conduct himself in this moment of triumph, as they had been in the moment of his humiliation. It is, however, needless to inform the friends of the Perpetual Curate that the anxious community gained very little by their curiosity. It was not the custom of the young Anglican to carry his personal feelings, either of one kind or another, into the pulpit with him, much less into the reading-desk, where he was the interpreter not of his own sentiments or emotions, but of common prayer and universal worship. Mr Wentworth did not even throw a little additional warmth into his utterance of the general thanksgiving, as he might have done had he been a more effusive man; but, on the contrary, read it with a more than ordinary calmness, and preached to the excited people one of those terse little unimpassioned sermons of his, from which it was utterly impossible to divine whether he was in the depths of despair or at the summit and crown of happiness. People who had been used to discover a great many of old Mr Bury's personal peculiarities in his sermons, and who, of recent days, had found many allusions which it was easy to interpret in the discourses of Mr Morgan, retired altogether baffled from the clear and succinct brevity of the Curate of St Roque's. He was that day in particular so terse as to be almost epigrammatic, not using a word more than was necessary, and displaying that power of saying a great deal more than at the first moment he appeared to say, in which Mr Wentworth's admirers specially prided themselves. Perhaps a momentary human gratification in the consciousness of having utterly baffled curiosity passed through the Curate's mind as he took off his robes when the service was over; but he was by no means prepared for the ordeal which awaited him when he stepped forth from the pretty porch of St Roque's. There his three aunts were awaiting him, eager to hear all about it, Miss Dora, for the first time in her life, holding the principal place. "We are going away to-morrow, Frank, and of course you are coming to lunch with us," said aunt Dora, clinging to his arm. "Oh, my dear boy, I am so happy, and so ashamed, to hear of it. To think you should be provided for, and nobody belonging to you have anything to do with it! I don't know what to say," said Miss Dora, who was half crying as usual; "and as for Leonora, one is frightened to speak to her. Oh, I wish you would say something to your aunt Leonora, Frank. I don't know whether she is angry with us or with you or with herself, or what it is; or if it is an attack on the nerves—though I never imagined she had any nerves; but, indeed, whatever my brother may say, it looks very like—dreadfully like—the coming-on of the Wentworth complaint. Poor papa was just like that when he used to have it coming on; and Leonora is not just—altogether—what you would call a female, Frank. Oh, my dear boy, if you would only speak to her!" cried Miss Dora, who was a great deal too much in earnest to perceive anything comical in what she had said.

"I should think it must be an attack on the

temper," said the Curate, who, now that it was all over, felt that it was but just his aunt Leonora should suffer a little for her treatment of him. "Perhaps some of her favourite colporteurs have fallen back into evil ways. There was one who had been a terrible blackguard, I remember. It is something that has happened among her mission people, you may be sure, and nothing about me."

"You don't know Leonora, Frank. She is very fond of you, though she does not show it," said Miss Dora, as she led her victim in triumphantly through the garden door, from which the reluctant young man could see Lucy and her sister in their black dresses just arriving at the other green door from the parish church, where they had occupied their usual places, according to the ideas of propriety which were common to both the Miss Wodehouses. Mr Wentworth had to content himself with taking off his hat to them, and followed his aunts to the table, where Miss Leonora took her seat much with the air of a judge about to deliver a sentence. She did not restrain herself even in consideration of the presence of Lewis the butler, who, to be sure, had been long enough in the Wentworth family to know as much about its concerns as the members of the house themselves, or perhaps a little more. Miss Leonora sat down grim and formidable in her bonnet, which was in the style of a remote period, and did not soften the severity of her personal appearance. She pointed her nephew to a seat beside her, but she did not relax her features, nor condescend to any ordinary preliminaries of conversation. For that day even she took Lewis's business out of his astonished hands, and herself divided the chicken with a swift and steady knife and anatomical precision; and it was while occupied in this congenial business that she broke forth upon Frank in a manner so unexpected as almost to take away his breath.

"I suppose this is what fools call poetical justice," said Miss Leonora, "which is just of a piece with everything else that is poetical—weak folly and nonsense that no sensible man would have anything to say to. How a young man like you, who know how to conduct yourself in some things, and have, I don't deny, many good qualities, can give in to come to an ending like a trashy novel, is more than I can understand. You are fit to be put in a book of the Good-child series, Frank, as an illustration of the reward of virtue," said the strong-minded woman, with a little snort of scorn; "and, of course, you are going to marry and live happy ever after, like a fairy tale."

"It is possible I may be guilty of that additional enormity," said the Curate, "which, at all events, will not be your doing, my dear aunt, if I might suggest a consolation. You cannot help such things happening, but, at least, it should be a comfort to feel you have done nothing to bring them about."

To which Miss Leonora answered by another hard breath of mingled disdain and resentment. "Whatever I have brought about, I have tried to do what I thought my duty," she said. "It has always seemed to me a very poor sort of virtue that expects a reward for doing what it ought to do. I don't say you haven't behaved very well in this business, but you've done nothing extraordinary; and why I should have rushed out of my way to reward you for it—Oh, yes, I know you did not expect anything," said Miss Leonora; "you have told me as much on various occasions, Frank. You have, of course, always been perfectly independent, and scorned to flatter your old aunts by any deference to their convictions; and, to be sure, it is nothing to you any little pang they may feel at having to dispose otherwise of a living that has always been in the family. You are of the latest fashion of Anglicanism, and we are only a parcel of old women. It was not to be expected that our antiquated ideas could be worth as much to you as a parcel of flowers and trumpery——"

These were actually tears which glittered in Miss Leonora's eyes of fiery hazel grey—tears of very diminutive size, totally unlike the big dew-drops which rained from Miss Dora's placid orbs and made them red, but did *her* no harm—but still a real moisture, forced out of a fountain which lay very deep down and inaccessible to ordinary efforts. They made her eyes look rather fiercer than otherwise for the moment; but they all but impeded Miss Leonora's speech, and struck with the wildest consternation the entire party at the table, including even Lewis, who stood transfixed in the act of drawing a bottle of soda-water, and, letting the cork escape him in his amazement, brought affairs to an unlooked-for climax by hitting Miss Wentworth, who had been looking on with interest without taking any part in the proceedings. When the fright caused by this unintentional shot had subsided, Miss Leonora was found to have entirely recovered herself; but not so the Perpetual Curate, who had changed colour wonderfully, and no longer met his accuser with reciprocal disdain.

"My dear aunt," said Frank Wentworth, "I wish you would not go back to that. I suppose we parsons are apt sometimes to exaggerate trifles into importance, as my father says. But, however, as things have turned out, I could not have left Carlingford," the Curate added, in a tone of conciliation; "and now, when good fortune has come to me unsought——"

Miss Leonora finished her portion of chicken in one energetic gulp, and got up from the table. "Poetic justice!" she said, with a furious sneer. "I don't believe in that kind of rubbish. As long as you were getting on quietly with your work I felt disposed to be rather proud of you, Frank. But I don't approve of a man ending off neatly like a novel in this sort of ridiculous way. When you succeed to the Rectory I suppose you will begin fighting, like the other man, with the new curate, for working in your parish?"

"When I succeed to the Rectory," said Mr Wentworth, getting up in his turn from the table, "I give you my word, aunt Leonora, no man shall work in *my* parish unless I set him to do it. Now I must be off to my work. I don't suppose Carlingford Rectory will be the end of me," the Perpetual Curate added, as he went away, with a smile which his aunts could not interpret. As for Miss Leonora, she tied her bonnet-strings very tight, and went off to the afternoon service at Salem Chapel by way of expressing her sentiments more forcibly. "I daresay he's bold enough to take a bishopric," she said to herself; "but fortunately we've got *that* in our own hands as long as Lord Shaftesbury lives;" and Miss Leonora smiled grimly over the prerogatives of her party. But though she went to Salem Chapel that afternoon, and consoled herself that she could secure the bench of bishops from any audacious invasion of Frank Wentworth's hopes, it is true, notwithstanding, that Miss Leonora sent her maid next morning to London with certain obsolete ornaments, of which, though the fashion was hideous, the jewels were precious; and Lucy Wodehouse had never seen anything so brilliant as the appearance they presented when they returned shortly after reposing upon beds of white satin in cases of velvet—"Ridiculous things," as Miss Leonora informed her, "for a parson's wife."

It was some time after this—for, not to speak of ecclesiastical matters, a removal, even when the furniture is left behind and there are only books, and rare ferns, and old china, to convey from one house to another, is a matter which involves delays—when Mr Wentworth went to the railway station with Mrs Morgan to see her off finally, her husband having gone to London with the intention of joining her in the new house. Naturally, it was not without serious thoughts that the Rector's wife left the place in which she had made her first beginning of active life, not so successfully as she had hoped. She could not help recalling, as she went along the familiar road, the hopes so vivid as to be almost certainties with which she had come into Carlingford. The long waiting was then over, and the much-expected era had arrived, and existence had seemed to be opening in all its fulness and strength before the two who had looked forward to it so long. It was not much more than six months ago; but Mrs Morgan had made a great many discoveries in the mean time. She had found out the wonderful difference between anticipation and reality; and that life, even to a happy woman married after long patience to the man of her choice, was not the smooth road it looked, but a rough path enough cut into dangerous ruts, through which generations of men and women followed each other without ever being able to mend the way. She was not so sure as she used to be of a great many important matters which it is a wonderful consolation to be certain of—but, notwithstanding, had to go on as if she had no doubts, though the clouds of a defeat, in which, certainly, no honour, though a good deal of the *prestige* of inexperience had been lost, were still looming behind. She gave a little sigh as she shook Mr Wentworth's hand at parting. "A great many things have happened in six months," she said—"one never could have anticipated so many changes in what looks so short a period of one's life"—and as the train which she had watched so often rushed past that bit of new wall on which the Virginian creeper was beginning to grow luxuriantly, which screened the railway from the Rectory windows, there were tears in Mrs Morgan's eyes. Only six months, and so much had happened!—what might not happen in all those months, in all those years of life which scarcely looked so hopeful as of old? She preferred turning her back upon Carlingford, though it was the least comfortable side of the carriage, and put down her veil to shield her eyes from the dust, or perhaps from the inspection of her fellow-travellers: and once more the familiar thought returned to her of what a different woman she would have been had she come to her first experiences of life with the courage and confidence of twenty or even of five-and-twenty, which was the age Mrs Morgan dwelt upon most kindly. And then she thought with a thrill of vivid kindness and a touch of tender envy of Lucy Wodehouse, who would now have no possible occasion to wait those ten years.

As for Mr Wentworth, he who was a priest, and knew more about Carlingford than any other man in the place, could not help thinking, as he turned back, of people there, to whom these six months had produced alterations far more terrible than any that had befallen the Rector's wife:—people from whom the light of life had died out, and to whom all the world was changed. He knew of men who had been cheerful enough when Mr Morgan came to Carlingford, who now did not care what became of them; and of women who would be glad to lay down their heads and hide them from the mocking light of day. He knew it, and it touched his heart with the tenderest pity of life, the compassion of happiness; and he knew too that the path upon which he was about to set out led through the same glooms, and was no ideal career. But perhaps because Mr Wentworth was young—perhaps because he was possessed by that delicate sprite more dainty than any Ariel who puts rosy girdles round the world while his time of triumph lasts—it is certain that the new Rector of Carlingford turned back into Grange Lane without the least shadow upon his mind or timidity in his thoughts. He was now in his own domains, an independent monarch, as little inclined to divide his power as any autocrat; and Mr Wentworth came into his kingdom without any doubts of his success in it, or of his capability for its government. He had first a little journey to make to bring back Lucy from that temporary and reluctant separation from the district which propriety had made needful; but, in the mean time, Mr Wentworth trode with firm foot the streets of his parish, secure that no parson nor priest should tithe or toll in his dominions, and a great deal more sure than even Mr Morgan had been, that henceforth no unauthorised evangelisation should take place in any portion of his territory. This sentiment, perhaps, was the principal difference perceptible by the community in general between the new Rector of Carlingford and the late Perpetual Curate of St Roque's.

THE END.

CPSIA information can be obtained
at www.ICGtesting.com
Printed in the USA
LVHW040024180422
716440LV00005B/439